A COMEDY OF BOATS

MEMOIRS OF A LAKE DISTRICT LAUNCH DRIVER

PETER MORRISON
and
PETER NOCK

ORINOCO PRESS

"A Comedy of Boating"

First Published in 1992 by:
Orinoco Press
41 Oakthwaite Road
Windermere
Cumbria LA23 2BD

Designed & printed by:
**Badger Press
Bowness-on-Windermere
Cumbria**

Copyright © P.J. Morrison 1992
© P.L. Nock 1992

ISBN 0 9514778 2 X

This book is sold subject to the condition that it shall not, by way of trade or otherwise, be lent, resold, hired out or otherwise circulated without the publisher's prior consent in any form of binding or cover other than that in which it is published and without a similar condition including this condition being imposed upon the subsequent purchaser.

"There is nothing, absolutely nothing, half so much fun as simply messing about in boats."

- Kenneth Grahame, *The Wind in the Willows*

Note from the Authors

It is usual, in works of fiction, to claim that the characters depicted bear no relation to any person living or dead. Such a claim is obviously fraudulent in a fictionalised autobiography such as the present publication. Nevertheless, the authors would hope that the many characters they encountered during their careers as skippers of commercial pleasure launches in the English Lakes would be complimented, rather than offended, should they succeed in recognising themselves in the following pages. Any such characters have been disguised as far as fiction will permit. No offence has been intended at any time to any person.

Birblemere is a fictional lake set in a real location, the English Lakes. The characters are fictional, the names of the boats are fictional. Some of the events described are fictional, some a mixture of fact and fiction, and some - perhaps even the more improbable ones - really did take place. It is up to our readers to guess which.

Acknowledgements

The authors' thanks are due to Mrs Dorothy Murdoch for her help in typing out an earlier version of this novel.

A COMEDY OF BOATING

CHAPTER 1.   A Driving Test on Water

"**THAT** idiot Locoweed! The cretin's just sunk another rowing boat - tipped 'em all into the water, and now the stupid so-and-so looks as if 'e's trying to reverse over them!"

The speaker was a swarthy, well-built gentleman in his mid-thirties, wearing an old raincoat and a broad-brimmed hat, and he was standing at the end of a short wooden pier gazing angrily over the crowded waters of Birblemere. He seemed hardly to notice me standing quietly at his elbow, although his words could be addressed to nobody else. I was also staring out across the lake, unable for the moment to make any sense of the confused scene in front of my eyes - boats of all shapes and sizes criss-crossing the crowded bay in a seemingly hazardous and pointless manner. I was to learn this was absolutely normal for a Saturday, or indeed for any other day of the week.

Who, I wondered, could this fellow Locoweed be? Surely not a launch driver - a man in sole charge of a pleasure craft carrying upwards of thirty people, all his sole responsibility, all decisions with regard to navigation his, and his alone? After all, when I'd applied for the job for which I was now supposed to be being interviewed, I had understood that only responsible and reasonably intelligent people would even be considered.

Locoweed, as they called the errant driver, seemed to be an exception. Captain Wright - for that was the name of the gentleman standing on the end of the pier - gestured in frustration at the uncontrollable antics of his employee, and finally turned to me.

"So you're Brian," he said.

"Yes," I replied.

"Well, we'll be needing a new driver this season, so let's see how you shape. I'd better introduce you to Tom, he'll take care of you." He turned and called across to an adjacent pier, where a number of small pleasure launches were moored. Cupping his hand to his mouth, he yelled, "Tom!"

In response to the call a man miraculously appeared from a seemingly empty cabin. Captain Wright beckoned him over, and a short while later he was standing beside us. Tom was a broad-shouldered, rather short, man in his early fifties. He wore a pair of Wellingtons, a navy sweater and a plain, peaked cap of a type favoured by nautical persons the world over. He looked rather disgruntled that his little nap had been interrupted.

"This is Brian," Captain Wright announced. "Take him out for some practice, will you? And whatever you do, keep away from Locoweed. Looks like 'e's just sunk another boat."

Tom nodded briefly to me. "C'mon," he muttered, and turned on his heel. I followed him round to the next pier in silence. Tom led the way onto his boat, leaping nimbly across a couple of launches moored side by side, stepping round and over the various obstacles which impeded his way, while I, not being quite as agile, tripped over a couple of seats, banged my head on a projecting roof, tangled my foot in a neat coil of rope and then kicked a metal bucket over with a resounding crash. Tom looked round reproachfully. By the time I had made my way over to the launch, Tom had the engine running, the fore and aft ropes cast off and neatly coiled and was waiting for his new apprentice, a mixture of resignation and bored contempt in his expression.

"Sorry," I said, thinking of the bucket and feeling I had not made a very good start. Tom said nothing. He cast off, put the boat into gear and reversed out into the bay, which was rather restricted at that point and necessitated a good deal of to-ing and fro-ing. Then he put the engine ahead and the little launch glided smoothly forward.

I looked about me with wonder. On our way out we met the launch which the man called Locoweed was driving, returning to port with a capsized rowing boat trailing behind and the dripping occupants standing around Locoweed gesticulating and speaking rather forcefully to him. Is this the usual state of affairs round here, I wondered, or have I witnessed some terrible accident? I saw the launch land and disgorge its party, to be met on the pier by Captain Wright who then led them all in the direction of the launch company office where, I imagined, the passengers would be placated and refunded, and Locoweed dismissed with ignominy.

That, I was to learn, was not the way the firm operated.

My thoughts were interrupted by Tom stopping the boat in midwater. "Right," he announced to his rather nervous pupil. "This is the wheel. Turn it to the right, the boat goes to the right. Turn to the left, the boat goes left. Here's the gear lever - push it forwards, the boat will go ahead. Push it back, the boat will go backwards. And this is the throttle - open it up, the boat goes faster. Put the boat into reverse to stop it. Got all that?"

I nodded dumbly, hardly able to comprehend all that information in one go. But I *did* notice that Tom disdained the various nautical expressions used on boats, such as port and starboard, ahead and astern.

"Right you are, young feller," Tom continued. "See that pier over there? Take the boat in and land there."

I peered in the indicated direction. Ahead there stood a row of rather dilapidated-looking boathouses which could all have done with a fresh coat of paint. It was here, I learned later, that the beautiful old Birblemere racing yachts used to be built, but were now used to store some of the pleasure launches during the winter. From each boathouse a rickety wooden pier projected into the lake, and it was next to one of these that I was required to land.

Good grief! I thought. Just like that? Concealing my dismay I stood behind the wheel and grasped it tightly with both hands. After a while, as nothing seemed to be happening, Tom said, "Go on then." The gear lever, I thought, and pushed it forward. Nothing happened. "Harder," said Tom.

I tried again, harder. Suddenly it moved, catching my knuckles a sharp crack as they came into contact with the engine casing. Tom had forgotten to warn me about that. But now the engine was in gear and - miracle of miracles - the boat was moving ahead. I gripped the wheel tighter. Which way?

"Faster," said Tom.

My other hand (the uninjured one) reached gingerly down to a little handle protruding from a small slot in the engine casing, which was the only thing that looked as if it might be a throttle, and pushed it down. The engine roared suddenly, and the boat shot forwards, the sudden acceleration almost sending me off balance. "Slacken off!" shouted Tom.

All at once we seemed to be alongside the pier, the huge doorway of the boathouse rushing towards us at a terrifying rate. With great presence of mind I pulled the gear lever back into neutral, the engine screamed as its revs built up, but no time to do anything about it, I had to stop before we splintered that door; I slammed the gear lever back, the engine screamed as the boat responded and we came to a halt, then started going backwards before I remembered to put the engine back into neutral. I had, amazingly, made a tolerable landing, and at the right pier as well. Feeling rather pleased with myself, I glanced round at my instructor.

"That was terrible," said Tom. "Back out and do it again." He was a hard task-master. I was made to do it again, and again, and yet again for a good hour or so, backing out and landing until I began to feel rather like a yo-yo. At last Tom said, "Right, that'll do. Take us back into the bay now."

Feeling a little more confident this time than I had when I first set out, I directed the launch back to where we had come from.

"And mind how you land against that other boat." warned Tom. "I don't want any scratches on his hull, or anything." And to emphasise his point, he secured a small tyre over the side to act as a fender. Heart beating, I managed a tolerable landing and Tom fastened up to the next launch.

"It's teatime now," he explained as we left the pier. I had managed to negotiate my way across the two other launches (which didn't seem to have moved since we had left over an hour ago), this time without tripping over anything. "Come down on Wednesday and take your test - oh, and you'd better learn these." He reached inside his jacket and handed me a dog-eared, coffee-stained booklet, which I absent-mindedly put away into my pocket.

Tom disappeared in the direction of the nearest café. I walked a short distance along the stony beach and gazed at the small launch I'd just been driving. She was a neat little boat of some thirty-five feet with a plain, varnished hull, and the name *Shelduck* clearly painted on her bows. Despite the bruised knuckles, I was beginning to like her; and this was just as well, because although I didn't yet know it, *Shelduck* was to be my command for the rest of that summer.

I'd better say a few words about myself at this point. I was a young man of some twenty years, of average height and appearance, and I'd only arrived in the Lakes the day before. This time last week I had been unemployed in London (resting between jobs, you might say) and at a bit of a loose end. An unexpected phone call from my aunt, who lived in the Lakes, revealed that there was a vacancy for a launch driver with the local pleasure boat company. I rang the number she gave me and was answered by Captain Wright in person, who told me to get up there right away. My one and only bag packed, the very next morning I was on an inter-city from Euston heading north at ninety miles an hour to a part of England I had never even gone near before.

The train deposited me at Bumblethwaite station, which is some distance from the lakeside village of Bulswick, where my aunt lived. On asking directions from one of the locals, I was regarded for a few seconds with a blank stare before he said, "Oh, it's Buzzock you want," and proceeded to direct me accordingly. I bet they have a lot of names round here which aren't pronounced as they're spelled, I told myself; I was right, too.

The village of Bulswick was charmingly situated beside a pleasant bay overlooking Birblemere, as the largest lake thereabouts was known. I was a newcomer to the countryside: my previous horizon had been tall buildings, offices, factories, city streets, my ears deafened by the roar of traffic. Birblemere came as a revelation to me: the wide expanse of open lake, the distant islands set against a backdrop of tree-clad slopes and lofty fells, the sunlight glittering on the gently rippling water - the entire scene on that spring morning was as bright and as clear as if it had been newly-painted. At that moment I felt like a watcher on a peak in Darien, a whole new world spread out before me; and fell in love with Birblemere there and then. I probably never fell out of love since.

Walking slowly back up the hill to my aunt's, I decided this was a wonderful place to work. I found myself whole-heartedly agreeing with the Water Rat, who said, "There is nothing, absolutely nothing, half so much fun as simply messing about in boats." When I got back I remembered the crumpled booklet Tom had given me, tucked away in my pocket and forgotten about. I took it out, spread it open on the bed, and began to read.

"BIRBLEMERE PILOTAGE HANDBOOK", ran the title on the cover, *"Issued by the Birblemere Navigation Board, and containing the Rules of Navigation and Advice to Pilots"*, along with a whole load of other pretentious stuff. Then perhaps, I thought, all was not chaos out there after all. Obviously every vessel was fully under command - Locoweed notwithstanding - and knew exactly where it was going and how to get there.

Section One dealt with lights:

"A power-driven vessel of fifteen feet or more in length, when under way, shall show:-

"In the forepart of the vessel where it can best be seen and at a height of not less than X feet above the hull and of not less than Y feet above the sidelights prescribed in paragraph 2 of this Rule, a white light so constructed and fixed as to show from right ahead to N degrees abaft the beam on both sides of the vessel, and of such a character as to be visible at a distance of at least M miles....." and so on.

Everybody, it would appear, had to have lights of one kind or another, all denoting different circumstances. Even rowing boats had to wave a coloured lantern at other boats.

Suppose, for instance, that I were piloting a vessel of more than X feet, towing one boat alongside and another astern, temporarily out of control and in the process of refuelling whilst under way. To explain all this at night would have required me to display more lights than Blackpool Tower.

The rules also told you how to pass other vessels:

"When two power-driven vessels are meeting end on, or nearly end on, so as to involve risk of collision, each shall alter her course to starboard, so that each may pass on the port side of the other."

What could be simpler? I thought. Having been an avid fan of Horatio Hornblower not too many years ago, I already knew what port and starboard meant.

The rules seemed to cater for every eventuality. They even prescribed, for instance, that a sailing cruiser pretending to be under sail, but actually having her engine running as well as her sails hoisted, was classed as a power-driven vessel, so there. And there was even a rule telling you to depart from the other rules if necessary - a neat little let-out, I thought.

I carried the Birblemere Pilotage Handbook about with me wherever I went, reading the Rules over and over again and repeating them to myself. They became, in a sense, my Bible, dominating my thoughts day and night. I would mutter them at the breakfast table, at the dinner table and the supper table until my aunt began to wish she had never invited me up to Bulswick. I repeated them when queueing in shops, startling assistants and shoppers alike by saying sternly: "No vessel shall proceed at a speed greater than ten statute miles per hour through the waters of Birblemere in the area bounded by a line drawn from Shuttleworth Nab to the south end of Ross Holme....." and so on.

The dreaded Day grew inexorably closer. I comforted myself with the knowledge that even if I had virtually no practical experience of launch handling, at least I knew the Rules - forwards, backwards and inside out.

It was a bright and sunny morning, only a light breeze playing over the water, practically ideal test conditions. I reported promptly to Captain Wright at 09.00 hours, who in turn sent me over to find Tom, who was busy cleaning the brasses.

"Morning, Tom!"

"Mornin'," Tom grunted. "Come for yer test, then? OK, let's 'ave a cup o' tea first."

"But..... won't we be late?" I enquired anxiously.

"Nay worry, lad. We never get there on time anyway."

He led the way into the nearby café and generously bought me a cup of tea. Half an hour later we were still drinking tea, and I was getting rather worried, wondering how the official who was going to conduct the test would react when nobody turned up for it. Just as I was about to put this point to my tutor, Tom replaced his cup and announced, "Right, lad. Let's go." And off we went.

The test was to be conducted by a Mr John Wall, who was described as a Lake Ranger - there's glory for you. The Ranger's boathouse lay further down the lake, and I had to drive *Shelduck* out round the long promontory of Shuttleworth Nab and into the next bay, Deansgate Wyke. We found Mr Wall in his office trying on a new uniform. He greeted Tom warmly and invited both of us in for a cup of tea. Mr Wall, as I later discovered, was in fact a retired boatman who had taken the job of Lake Ranger because the duties were few and he could spend the entire day in a nice warm office without actually having to do much cruising around on the lake - what's more, the uniform came free. When he *did* have to go out, a fast patrol boat was provided (also free), of which he was just a teensy bit frightened.

The tea over, all three of us started down the pier. I was by now scared stiff and shaking like a jelly - after all, driving a boat is not like driving a car, at least in the latter case you have a reasonable idea where you're going. Not so on water. What's more, with all those cups of tea my bladder was beginning to feel uncomfortably full.

"Right," the Ranger said brightly. "Brian, is it? Take her out, Brian, and then come back in for a landing at this pier, could you please?" Not waiting for a reply, he turned and ducked into the cabin to sit down and continue his conversation with Tom. The way they were chatting, you'd think they'd never seen each other for years. I struggled to reverse the boat through the confusing maze of moored cruisers which infested this part of Deansgate Wyke, and eventually by pure luck found myself on the open lake. Then it was time to go back in again. Weaving round the various mooring buoys, dodging the waiting cruisers, I sneaked a glance over my shoulder at the occupants of the diminutive cabin, but Tom and the Ranger were still deep in conversation and taking no notice of me whatsoever.

Miraculously I managed to land the boat without bumping the pier, edging cautiously in to take advantage of the calm weather, tied up, switched the engine off and stood in the cabin doorway, wondering what to do next. They were still talking. I coughed discreetly.

The Ranger looked up. "Ah, we're back. Well done. Let's go into the office."

We all trooped back into the office. Once Mr Wall was safely reinstalled at his desk, he commenced shuffling through a large file of papers, looking for the appropriate form to fill in. Was that it? I asked myself. What about all those navigation rules? As if in answer to the unspoken query the Ranger asked, without looking up, "Do you know where the rock markers are?"

Good Lord, I thought. There must be millions. Out of the corner of my eye, I saw Tom nod.

"Yes," I said.

"Good," remarked the Ranger, found the form, and began to fill it in. I then had to sign it, pay the appropriate fee, and lo! I was now a fully licensed, paid-up boatman. I was given a plastic tag to pin to my jersey proclaiming to the world at large that the bearer was licensed by Birblemere Navigation Board to take charge of and navigate a launch plying commercially for hire on the waters of the said lake. And that was that. All that time spent learning the rules was now water under the bridge, so to speak.

I thanked the Ranger, dived thankfully into the loo to get rid of all that tea, then piloted *Shelduck* back to Bulswick while Tom lounged in the cabin studying the racing page of his newspaper. Once in port I proudly took my license up to Captain Wright, who carefully filed it away in a drawer and placed me on the payroll.

"You start tomorrow," he announced. "You'll be driving *Shelduck*."

Shelduck! I was overjoyed. My command, my responsibility..... my baby. So my life as a boatman had begun. At that young and tender age, I had no idea just how long and eventful a life that would be; for what I thought was just a seasonal job turned out to be a lifetime's profession.

CHAPTER 2. Learning the Ropes

I very soon discovered that it was not enough just to pass the test. There was a formidable quantity of knowledge which I had to acquire before I could even begin to think of calling myself a boatman, and my first week was spent mainly in going on cruises with Tom - and one or two others - to learn the various routes which were taken round the lake. Cruises went out to every part of Birblemere - to the head of the lake at Boxingdale, to Biskey Landing at its foot, together with trips of varying complexity taking in some of the many small islands which adorn the lake between Bulswick and Boxingdale. There was also a "Sunset Cruise", the class trip of the day which was timed to catch post-prandial strollers from the big hotels and whisk them away to contemplate the splendours of a Lakeland sunset - very nice if it didn't happen to be raining, as it often was.

One morning during my first week I was busy pumping *Shelduck*'s bilges out when I was called over by Captain Wright and introduced to David Duckworth. David was a tall, rather serious young man not much older than me, who had worked with the firm for a number of years and was in charge of a huge, gleaming launch called *Mallard*, which I suppose you could describe as the flagship of our little fleet.

David was busy cleaning and polishing his cabin windows.

"Morning," I said, somewhat diffidently. "Anything I can do to help?"

David paused and glared at me suspiciously. "Yes," he said at last. "Go and have a cup of tea, and come back five minutes before we're due to sail."

These boatmen were men of few words, I was finding. If I wanted to discover anything at all about the job, I'd have to learn to use my eyes rather than ask my new colleagues. I watched David from the window of the café; having conveniently got rid of his unwanted crew, David simply carried on cleaning. *Mallard* was his pride and joy, he didn't want strangers setting foot on that sacred deck. He took his job very seriously, which was not surprising since his father was the semi-retired chairman of the firm, and David was in line to inherit a substantial share of the business when his father passed on. 'Chairman Fred' was how the other drivers referred to Duckworth senior, and he was reckoned to be a typical boatman of the 'old school', assuming anyone knew what was meant by that expression. Perhaps he was into flogging and keel-hauling if any of his employees offended.

Anyway, I reported back half an hour later (strange how we always seemed to be drinking cups of tea in this job), the boat left on time, and *Mallard* with a dozen or so passengers slipped gracefully out of the bay and headed west for Biskey Landing. We passed the grandiose Devonshire Hotel, then the row of old boathouses where I had gone practising with Tom, and reached Shuttleworth Nab where the speed limit ended and David could open up the throttle.

The engine note increased significantly, the bows rose up in the air, and *Mallard* headed for the open lake, a deep wash fanning out astern of us. David explained to me that he had to travel fairly fast in order to get back on time, as it was a good distance to Biskey. Soon the mysterious island of Ross Holme was left astern and we were passing the well-wooded Birblemere shoreline. In this neck of the woods, if you'll pardon the expression, the trees are many and the inhabitants few. There really was very little to see except trees, I wondered what the passengers had paid their money for. David passed the time by pointing out the various islands we passed - especially Sedge Holme which had an unmarked channel round it, known only to the local boatmen (and perhaps a few fishermen) but not to anyone else - which was why, every other time you passed it, you'd see one of the local hire cruisers well and truly aground. They'd usually been there several hours as this was an unfrequented part of the lake, and were desperately calling for a tow off. David usually smiled and looked the other way. I discovered that he didn't have a very high opinion of holiday-makers.

Just under an hour later we arrived at Biskey Landing (I never did find out why it had this curious name), where David berthed at a small jetty. On the other side of this jetty the Biskey launch, *Bananas*, was moored. Once disembarked, our flock were shepherded across to a nearby café, where morning coffee and biscuits were waiting. David took me round the back and introduced me to the kitchen staff, where we were fed and watered free of charge. They were no doubt grateful for the large party we had brought down for them, and I was suitably impressed.

Refreshments over, we said goodbye and went back to the beach to wait for our passengers, who had all been carefully warned what time *Mallard* was due to leave. There was a line of rowing boats, all neatly painted in different colours, pulled up against the shore, all seeming to compete as to which could make the prettiest reflection in the still water.

David strolled over to chat with two of the boatmen who worked at this end of the lake - George Merryweather and Charlie Charcake. George was a wrinkled old fellow who looked as old as his boats, his face seamed and tanned to a high gloss just like a varnished plank. He'd worked down there all his life, David informed me later, and wouldn't even dream of retiring. Ten out of ten for continuity, I thought.

Charlie was a good bit younger, and drove the *Bananas* when there were enough passengers for it, which wasn't very often. He had an artificial arm which was permanently bent at the elbow in the manner of a waiter at a better class hotel. There was a twisted smile on his lips and a tame jackdaw on his shoulder. This sagacious fowl lived nearby and had adopted Charlie, perching on his crooked arm at mealtimes to be fed. Charlie had taught it various obscenities over the years, which it would repeat loudly and clearly from time to time, much to the consternation of female customers who thought it was Charlie himself who was addressing them.

There were many stories circulating about Charlie, most of them apocryphal. One of the more interesting ones was that he was an unfrocked padre, dismissed from his order because of his disproportionate interest in the product of Scottish distilleries. Charlie himself would neither deny nor confirm the story.

When the passengers had boarded and been counted to ensure no-one was missing, we set off again for Bulswick, this time via the opposite side of the lake. We were five minutes late setting off, but David explained he always allowed for this, because however much he stressed the time of departure, somebody would invariably turn up late. Sure enough, right at the very last minute when the engine was running and David was standing holding the rope and pretending to look impatient, someone came charging down the beach, waving and shouting. "Hold on a minute! I'm just coming!" Then, as they were climbing aboard, "Sorry I'm late, didn't realise what time it had got to." David smiled mirthlessly and said nothing. They do it all the time, he said, there's always someone who has to be last.

The next day Tom grabbed me and took me out in *Shelduck* for some further practice, "wrecking the pier" as he expressed it, and on our return Captain Wright called me over to berth *Shelduck* alongside the main jetty ready to take the next cruise - "next to t' beck", as the boatmen termed it.

Well, I thought, I suppose he knows what he's doing. I wish I did. Had I done everything? Quickly I ran once more over the daily routine which Tom had dinned into me until I knew it forwards, backwards and sideways as well. Engine - checked. Fuel tanks - checked. Bilges pumped out - affirmative. Grease nipples - tightened. Ropes - neatly coiled away. Everything in order except for butterflies in the stomach and a rising sense of panic.

Passengers began to filter aboard *Shelduck* in twos and threes. Anxiously I scanned their faces: please God they all sit still, I prayed. There are many ways of dealing with one's passengers. They vary from one driver who treated them as if they were raw recruits to an army, practically marching them down the pier and embarking them by numbers, to the driver who would grovel to them in a manner so obsequious that he wore the knees out of two or three pairs of trousers each season. The fellow Locoweed, I was to discover, was a very good example of the latter.

You had to get used to being in the public eye. When backing out from the pier you have to face backwards - sorry, astern! - in order to see where you're going, and the very first thing to confront you is the concentrated stare of dozens of eyeballs, all watching your every move. This can be a little disconcerting, especially for beginners. One driver covered his confusion by whistling piercingly and tunelessly; another might go bright red and pretend to be admiring the scenery. I had to learn how to cope.

When there were about fifteen or twenty people on board, Captain Wright turned and performed a curious gesture: he waved both hands palm downwards in my direction, for all the world as if he were bowling underarm with both arms at once. I'm afraid this utterly incomprehensible gesture completely threw me. I glanced round for help. Tom was waiting nearby.

"What's he doing?" I asked.

"That's the go-away sign," he replied. "It's time for you to be on your way."

I climbed on board my boat, trying to look as though I'd been doing it for years, and started the engine.

"Don't worry," Tom said loudly for the benefit of the passengers. "Just remember to keep away from the red buoys, and if you get lost send us a postcard."

Having ruined the image I was trying to create he grinned, and helped me cast off the breast rope which secured the boat to the pier. Averting my head to hide the blushes, I put the gear lever into reverse. We moved slowly away from the pier, described the necessary semi-circle to get the bows pointing outwards, went into neutral, then into a forward, a touch of throttle, and we were on our way. Past the row of boathouses, past Shuttleworth Nab, smiling furiously at the passengers to fill them with confidence, Ross Holme now looming up...... *Good grief!* I'd forgotten to switch the fuel over! Hastily I lifted the engine case lid, turned a small valve on the fuel feeder lines, and wiped the sweat from my brow.

The reason for this little manoeuvre was that *Shelduck* was powered by the old-fashioned type of engine which used petrol and paraffin. The engine ran on paraffin while it was warm because it was cheaper, but when cold it had to be started using petrol. This meant the boat had to be equipped with a tiny tank holding about a gallon of petrol, and a huge fuel tank containing paraffin, otherwise known as Tractor Vaporising Oil, or TVO. You therefore had to switch over from petrol to TVO as soon as the engine was warm, and then back again before stopping, in order to make sure the carburettor contained petrol ready for starting again from cold. If the driver forgot to switch over to TVO once he was out on the lake (and this in fact happened quite frequently) the boat would sail gracefully along until about halfway round the cruise, when the engine would cough a few times and stop abruptly, leaving the boat drifting along at an ever-decreasing velocity in a most embarrassing silence. That would wake the driver up in a hurry, and if he had sufficient presence of mind he would immediately set upon the engine with a spanner, surreptitiously switching over to TVO as he did so, and with any luck the engine would be hot enough to start immediately. Thus he could turn defeat into victory, for the passengers would all think him an expert mechanic.

Well, I managed to escape that particular trap, and even navigated my way round a few of the islands uneventfully, mainly because we didn't meet any other craft to collide with, and continued cruising the prescribed fifty yards off the shore, hoping against hope that no other vessel - especially yachts - would get in the way. Birblemere was mercifully quiet that morning, they must have known I was coming. The loneliness of command gripped me. If anything were to happen, either on or off the boat, if anyone so much as asked a simple question, the decision was mine, the ultimate responsibility mine alone. Every soul on board was directly under my care, whether they knew it or not. Nothing, but nothing, must go wrong.

Fortunately nothing did, and presently I found myself threading my way back to Bulswick, this time from the opposite end. I slowed down, remembered to switch back from TVO to petrol, and lined up for my landing approach. As usual there was a small crowd of idlers and off-duty drivers waiting for the boat to land, as though they could sense that some catastrophe might provide them with free entertainment. I didn't disappoint them. I missed the pier by yards, the boatmen all laughed in glee and I had to reverse out, line up and try again. This time I made it, willing hands making a well-timed grab at the rope to tie up for me. The passengers disembarked looking relieved. In this way I completed one cruise and two landings.

I thought then that this might be it for the moment, I could go and get a cup of tea. But no - I was ordered to berth *Shelduck* alongside the loading position right away for yet another cruise. Someone intimated to me that Captain Wright thought I would need the practice.

It was during a slack moment later that day, after yet another failed landing, that one of the latter's assistants took the opportunity to wander down the pier. "What's up then?" he asked. "Want us to shift the pier sideways for you?"

"I'm very sorry," I said humbly. "It's my first day out."

He grinned good-humouredly and told me not to worry, nobody's perfect. This individual was, I learned, one of the boatmen of the older generation. His name was Bill Birblethwaite, he'd worked on the boats all his life except for a short break serving King and Country (we were never sure whether this was the Boer War or the First World War). From there he returned victorious and with an artificial leg, having left his real one on some foreign field. He walked with a limp, but could leap about nimbly enough from boat to boat, especially when chasing cheeky schoolboys, who sometimes came down to help when things got busy.

Bill Birblethwaite was a raconteur par excellence, forever coming out with little anecdotes about the lake or other boatmen he had known. His lips seldom stopped moving, and it didn't take long before you realised that most of what he said was absolute rubbish, and all invented in any case. I never grew tired of watching credulous visitors listen to old Bill with something approaching veneration as he babbled his meaningless drivel at them, every item accepted as a gem of local lore.

"Cormorants early this year," he'd remark. "In for a wet winter." Or: "Chestnut tree out in March, it'll be a hot 'un." Everyone seemed to believe him, perhaps he even believed it himself. It probably made their day if a couple of visitors could pass an hour or two chatting to Bill. They'd take his photograph, and you could see the almost childlike wonder in their eyes as they drank in his every word, imagining how they'd boast afterwards to their friends how much they'd learned about Birblemere from this marvellous old character they'd come across.

For all I know, Bulswick might once have been full of people like Bill Birblethwaite, but he turned to out to be the sole survivor of a once numerous breed and now, alas, facing extinction. There will be more about Bill later on.

CHAPTER 3. Sailing, and other Misadventures

DURING those early weeks on Birblemere I slowly began to gain confidence about piloting *Shelduck* on her various cruises. Since she was a fairly small launch she didn't go out a great deal, and I spent most of my time getting to know my fellow drivers, and how the firm worked. We've already met Tom, my instructor, and David Duckworth, the firm's number one driver, and I'll be introducing some of the others in due course. The managing director was Captain Wright, and it came as a bit of a shock to learn, after a few months in the firm's employ, that in fact his real name was Wainwright, and they only referred to him as Captain Wright because he was never wrong. You know the kind of person - you meet them in all walks of life. However, I have to say that he and I got on reasonably well together and we never had serious disagreements, such as would from time to time take place between him and the fellow Locoweed.

I never did discover if Locoweed was his first name, his nickname or his surname - anyway, it doesn't matter. This was the driver whom I'd seen on my very first day apparently reversing over a rowing boat. This kind of behaviour, I'm sorry to say, was fairly typical of Locoweed: if he wasn't colliding with a rowing boat he was having an argument with a yacht or a cabin cruiser, or running his launch aground, or breaking down in the middle of the lake through lack of fuel. He was a fellow - and they get them in every firm - who was prone to disaster. They couldn't sack him because he actually owned a few shares in the business.

At the time I began working for them, Bulswick & Lake Launch Services Ltd. was only just expanding from being a small family concern to a major commercial undertaking. However, that still lay some distance in the future. In those days everything was very informal, nobody seemed to bother much about anything. I suppose we operated to some kind of routine - arriving at work any time after nine o'clock, checking the engine, pumping the bilges, sweeping the floor - sorry, I mean deck - fuelling up, and this would bring us to the first tea break of the day, usually around ten.

There was a small café conveniently situated near the waterfront and facing out over the lake, and we all used to congregate here for our tea-breaks, and all kinds of other breaks as well, because from our favourite table near the window we could see whose boat was being loaded for the next cruise, and what time it was due to leave -

not that any of our cruises actually left on time, but all the same it was as well to be found hovering somewhere in the vicinity of the pier around the scheduled departure time.

The café was run by a Mrs Isadora Bardell, whom we all knew as Dora. A warm-hearted, cheerful lady, she would come down on wet days and open up especially for the boatmen, since she knew we'd be practically her only customers. She served us with endless cups of tea, often staying open well into the evening if it was fine day; and if the weather was cold, Dora would make soup to warm us all up. As if that wasn't generous enough, she charged a special low rate for boatmen, so that we practically monopolised her premises, and Dora's café became in fact the staff canteen. If ever the management wanted one of us in a hurry, they only had to poke a head round the door and yell "*Mallard!*" or "*Shelduck!*" and the driver whose boat was called would come running.

Speaking of management, I found the upper hierarchy of the firm rather confusing to begin with. In overall charge there was a Chairman Duckworth, David's father, a semi-mythical being whose name was whispered in awe and reverence, and who hardly ever came down to the lake. When he did, a mysterious silence would fall over the older boatmen; from this I deduced that Chairman Duckworth in his day had been an employer of a somewhat strict nature. Now, thankfully, he was semi-retired, and all executive power - ie. the day-to-day running of the firm - was vested in Captain Wright - the gentleman who'd engaged me in the first place

But it was not quite as simple as that. There were several individuals who worked with the firm - men who held a few shares, such as Locoweed, men who owned their own boats, or even fleets of boats, and they all came together every season to pool their resources, and split up again at the end. They all, without exception, wielded some measure of executive power according to how many boats they owned, and don't imagine everything was peace and harmony down there on the beach. Everyone wanted a thing doing his particular way, and they all had different ideas of how it was to be done, so there were frequent quarrels and raised voices on the beach. I was told that in the old days they even used to have fist fights. At the particular time I joined the firm there was one individual in particular, Captain Wright, who was slowly but surely gathering a power base and assuming some kind of ascendancy over the other boatmen. He was able to do this because he had the backing - financial as well as moral - of Chairman Fred himself.

My collective employers, it turned out, were rather unfortunately named, due to the acronym formed from the firm's trading title of 'Bulswick And Lake Launch Services'. The name had already been registered with the Board of Trade, and registration fees paid, before the blunder was discovered, by which time it was too late - they weren't going fork out another hefty fee just to change their name.

If you think that was funny, spare a thought for the rival firm who operated from Boxingdale, at the other end of the lake. Resulting from the amalgamation of the local bus company and the motor launches - the original idea being to provide a launch/bus service for outlying hamlets dotted around Birblemere - they had come up with the howler of 'Boxingdale United Motor Services'. I think the two names nicely complemented each other.

Speaking of Boxingdale reminds me of one event, only the second or third week after I'd started work, which will remain vividly in my mind for all time: fear has that effect. There I was, cruising along on the smooth and untroubled waters of Birblemere, minding my own business and thinking all was well with the world when all at once, quite out of the blue, I was overtaken at tremendous speed by the biggest launch I had ever seen in my life.

It was ten times the size of my little *Shelduck* which was lost in its shadow, and it roared by so close that the gap between us could be measured in millimetres. I could hear the roar of its mighty diesel engine above the purr of my TVO one, and I'm certain I felt the wind of its passage. My passengers stared up at his in disbelief, his passengers stared down at mine; one of them even volunteered a wave.

I found myself looking up at the wheelhouse where a huge, brass-bound wheel was in the grasp of a pair of enormous hands. The driver dwarfed me physically as his boat dwarfed mine. Six foot six if an inch, broad-shouldered and so well built as to appear almost fat in spite of his height, he towered above me, a great, gold-toothed grin of contempt on his swarthy, mocking features.

The huge launch swept past and I felt *Shelduck* lift on his stern wave. Up we went, higher and higher, and just as I was beginning to think it would never end the bows plummetted down, down we went, and hit the water with an almighty splash, soaking us all. There were lesser waves after this, and as I paused to wipe the spray from my face I saw the leering face of the enormous skipper peering round the outside of his cabin with a rope in his hand, in the contemptuous offer of a tow.

You porker! I thought. Good job I'd hit that wash end on and not broadside on, otherwise we'd have been sunk. Who on earth was the fellow, and what the hell did he think he was playing at? My passengers were still mopping themselves down and wringing out sodden handkerchiefs, etc, when the offending launch had disappeared round the next headland.

I learned on my return to Bulswick that the launch was *Pride of Raasay*, so named after her Highland builders, and she was the flagship of Boxingdale United Motor Services. The largest launch then operating on Birblemere, she could have carried little *Shelduck* as a lifeboat. The giant at the wheel was one William Clovis FitzMaurice, the son of a local landed gentleman who had long since abandoned trying to teach his errant offspring how to behave as a human being. William Clovis FitzMaurice was known the lake over as Boxer Bill, the Beast of Boxingdale.

"But what could I do?" I complained to Tom on getting back to port. "How can I stop myself and everyone else getting soaked when this monster roars by?"

"Nay, lad," was Tom's reply. "Turn your bows at right angles to 'is wash when you see 'im coming.... you'll learn 'ow to get out of 'is way in time. We all 'ave to."

"But can't the Lake Ranger do anything about him?"

"John Wall? 'E wouldn't dare lift 'is little finger when Boxer's around."

And that, it seemed, was the way things stood. Boxer was the king of Birblemere, and made it his pleasure to terrorise the entire lake. He enjoyed harassing, intimidating and panicking anyone unlucky enough to be near him in a boat. *Pride of Raasay* was the perfect weapon for this kind of terror tactic, and the pair made a formidable combination.

For instance, if Boxer had to return empty from Bulswick, having just conveyed a coach party there, he would cruise slowly back up the middle of the lake and then hover like a hunting hawk just short of where our launches used to cross over. You could see him lurking for miles away, but you *had* to cross at some point, and when you'd got halfway over the bows of the *Pride* would come hurtling towards you, raised high in the air as her stern bit down with the speed, Boxer would flash by grinning from ear to ear as you tried desperately to dodge before the wave hit.

This was called "giving a back-ender". His timing and boatmanship, it has to be said, were faultless. I once tried struggling into waterproofs when I saw Boxer approaching, but soon gave it up. There just wasn't time before the wave hit, and the passengers would look at you in astonishment. But when Boxer had gone, they'd wish they'd brought their waterproofs too!

When Boxer was in a particularly malignant mood, it was wonderful to see him cutting up a yacht race.

Birblemere had a wide variety of yacht and sailing clubs, and at weekends (often just between opening hours) they all raced different varieties of yachts, dinghies and other assorted sailing craft. As you might expect, there were numerous "misunderstandings" between yachtsmen and launch drivers. Since we were always on the lake, they couldn't go out without meeting a launch, and sometimes (in fact quite often) that launch would get in their way. From the launch driver's point of view, the yachts were getting in *his* way, and consequently both sides thought the other was doing it on purpose.

There are, of course, many occasions when manoeuvring a sailing boat out of the way of another vessel is very difficult. The sailor has to use wind alone to aid him, and if he's racing, he's extremely reluctant to give way and thus risk losing place by doing so. In addition he has to watch his sails, watch the wind, handle his boat accordingly, as well as try to see where he's going and what the other boats are doing. This isn't easy, and a yacht is not an ideal platform for viewing the surrounding lake for a full $360°$.

Compared with that, a launch driver can usually see all around him, is travelling at a constant speed regardless of wind direction, and can hold a more or less steady course. However, it's never easy to guess what a sailing vessel is going to do, and if the launch driver makes a wrong decision the two boats are going to get in each other's way, to their mutual annoyance. If it's a windy day the yachts may be moving as fast as, or even faster than a launch, making it almost impossible to get away. Launches, after all, are larger than yachts, and not as manoeuvrable as they appear to be.

Yes, I remembered all those navigation rules, they catered admirably for a one-to-one situation, but during races the lake gets so crowded that at peak times the rules can't always be applied to every boat in the vicinity all at once. Even if everyone were fully conversant with all the navigation rules and were doing their damndest to get it right, the whole situation is still open to individual interpretation. Amateur boating enthusiasts are rarely expert since they don't have enough time to spend on their hobby, they always have their hands full concentrating on their own vessel to the exclusion of everything else.

We always tried to go round yacht races where possible, rather than through them. Nothing seems to annoy the sailors more than a launch steaming though their midst! However, when a race is spread out right across the lake - Birblemere gets very narrow in places - the launch will just have to go through them. Obviously the driver cannot deviate so far from his allotted course as to make a nonsense of the cruise. Under these circumstances the other boatmen advised me to head for the biggest gap in the line and hope it was wide enough. Very comforting.

Racing yachts have a habit of rounding differently coloured buoys which are strategically placed round the lake on predetermined courses. If you can learn these, and so guess where the yachts are going, it can be a help. Here's a typical situation which I encountered one Saturday afternoon:

I was proceeding on my lawful business (as incidentally I had been when overtaken by Boxer) when to my horror I spotted a score of racing yachts bearing down on my starboard bow on what would be a collision course a quarter of a mile ahead if nothing happened meanwhile. I couldn't keep inshore of them in case they held course and trapped me; they covered practically the full width of the lake, so I couldn't go round them. Doing a 'U' turn and going back the way I'd just come was unthinkable; stopping my engine and just drifting around until they'd all sorted themselves out was a coward's way out. No - there was no alternative but to keep on going and dodge and weave my way around them as best as I could - unless they go round that next buoy.

"Please, oh please go round the buoy," I prayed. "Please God send them round the buoy" - hoping for divine intervention. Then: "Go round that buoy, you porkers." My brain hummed like a vast calculating machine, busily computing courses, speeds, distances, while at the same time trying telepathically to will the leader to turn.

Just at that moment an American tourist came up to me. "Say, whaat's that caastle?" he exclaimed, pointing to some nearby Victorian residence with mock battlements.

Stifling an urge to give up and jump overboard I started to explain. "That is Rosthwaite Keep. It was built in the 16th century to protect the farmers from border cattle raiders, but by Wordsworth's time it was used as a base for cat-gaffing[1] operations. It now belongs

---

[1]Cat-gaffing started as a rather tasteless joke. The idea was to convince visitors that as a pastime the locals would gather one morning armed with billhooks, spikes and other offensive instruments and set off round the local lanes, beating the extensive hedgerows ('thratching' is the correct expression) with their billhooks, etc. in the hope of catching a cat. The unfortunate creature would then be despatched

to the mountain rescue and they use it as a lighthouse to help climbers find their way down when they're lost on the fells."

He stared in wonder. "Say, ain't that swell then?" and ambled back to communicate this pack of lies to his wife. By this time the yachts had reached the buoy and were turning round it, so the crisis had been averted - at least until next time.

In addition to yachts, most of these sailing clubs ran dinghies, of which there appeared to be dozens of different classes, all much more of a problem. They tend to sail all crowded together, shouting technicalities at each other, such as: "Water! Water!" meaning not that they are dying of thirst in a desert (how could they be with millions of gallons of the stuff all around them?) but, "Get out of my way, you peasant!" Or: "Lee ho!" which was sometimes answered by, "Leo? No, he's not on this boat." Other popular cries included: "Splice your luff!" or "Reef the scuppers!" I always thought "Shiver your timbers!" ought to come into it as well, it sounds so professional.

I was in the Black Cormorant[2], the boatmen's local, one evening when I happened to encounter a dinghy sailor. After a few beers he volunteered the information that some of them find it great fun to harass launches wherever and whenever they can, since having priority of way they know what a nuisance they can make of themselves, and also how easy it is to terrify a new driver out of his wits.

It was not surprising, then, that sailing dinghies bore the brunt of Boxer Bill's rather individual brand of humour. He had a habit of bearing down on them flat out, made absolutely no attempt whatever to go round them but would zig-zag crazily through their midst, employing his admittedly superb boat-handling ability to scatter dinghies left, right and centre, leave masts see-sawing crazily from side to side, all chaos and confusion in his wake.

On one memorable occasion which had a great deal to do with

---

and left for dead by the roadside, for no other object than sheer sadistic fun.
A group of locals, tongue in cheek, were boasting in the pub one night about their arrangements for a cat-gaffing expedition the next day, hoping to impress and appal some visitors who could not help overhearing.
Unfortunately they were hoist with their own petard. Early the next morning some of these locals were woken at an early hour by a posse of RSPCA inspectors and policemen; and they had a very difficult job convincing the officers that it was all a bit of a leg-pull.
On the other hand, you'd think the officers would have realised they don't have roadside hedges in the Lakes, they have stone walls.

[2]Actually, we boatmen had a somewhat more colloquial expression for this hostelry.

Boxer's early retirement, a vast fleet of sailing vessels - ranging from great sailing yachts down to tiny dinghies - were all lined up ready for the most important race of the season, the prestigious Birblemere Cup. Someone must have done something to upset him, because suddenly Boxer came flying out from behind a small island where he had been concealed, screamed round the corner on two wheels (so to speak) tore across the front of the line flat out, and disappeared round another island in a cloud of exhaust smoke.

The confusion was magnificent. Masts began a merry dance between heaven and hell and back again, spars snapped, rigging was carried away, yachtsmen stood up to bellow indignation and wave fists, only to grab a rail to avoid being pitched overboard, the starter fired his pistol at *Pride of Raasay* in impotent fury. It was quite some time before order was restored, and they say the telephone line to Boxingdale United Motor Services was red-hot for hours afterwards.

The other factor which finally precipitated Boxer's abrupt departure was when he chased a catamaran which had had the temerity to sail across his bows. The catamaran raced for the safety of Bogholme Bay; and throwing caution to the winds, into Bogholme Bay Boxer pursued him.

The one thing which the other boatmen stressed to me, after I'd passed my test and started taking cruises on the lake, was: *never, never, never* under any circumstances go into Bogholme Bay. The reason was quite simple. Although having an inviting opening like the mouth of a broad and pleasant river, the unwary mariner who ventures within finds himself in a shallow bay filled with wicked rocks which lurk uncharted just below the surface, ready to rip the bottom out of a boat.

In addition there are a number of reeds and other aquatic growths, nodding in the wind or waving gently in the water, ready to foul a propeller. Bogholme Bay was the subject of many a tale of boats lost or sunk without trace; wise boatmen steered well clear of the place.

Boxer tore into this evil place at full speed intent only on his prey, confident in his knowledge of where the safe channels were to be found. On his first pass he failed to notice the catamaran taking shelter behind a clump of reeds, and miraculously managed to avoid running aground. Then he attempted another run (remember that all this charging about was taking place with a party of passengers on board who were supposed to be taking a pleasure cruise, not re-enacting the Battle of Trafalgar), churning the water into a turbid current of mud and weeds, and on this second run the bows of *Pride* rose high out of the water as she met her own wash and then crashed down onto a submerged reef.

Those wicked fangs of rock ripped the bottom half out of her, bent her propeller shaft in half, the water rushed in, *Pride* foundered and began to go down. It was so shallow here that when she could sink no further and was resting fair and square on the bottom her cabin was still above the surface.

At first the passengers didn't notice what had happened. They thought their launch had merely suffered engine failure (a frequent happening in those days). Then one of their number who happened to be a retired naval officer noticed the deck was awash. With great presence of mind he clambered up onto the cabin roof where the life-saving equipment was kept and began throwing life rings and buoyancy tanks into the lake with great enthusiasm, for people to hold onto when they abandoned ship. His efforts were somewhat beside the point as Boxer hadn't the slightest intention of getting wet. He hauled all his passengers up onto the roof and there they sat, watching the life belts float gently away.

Meanwhile the fellow in the catamaran, hardly believing his good luck in managing to flee from Boxer, took the opportunity to make good his escape to Boxingdale, where he reported what he had just seen. Imagine the panic! Men ran up and down the beach, shouting, starting up launches, casting off; and when the flotilla of rescue craft arrived at Bogholme, carefully nosing their way in through those treacherous waters, all they could see was the cabin roof of *Pride of Raasay* perched above water while all the passengers sat round in a group with Boxer conducting them in an improvised chorus of *"She'll be coming round the mountain when she comes!"*

They were presently rescued, restored to dry land, refunded, and treated to mugs of warming tea. In the confusion Boxer took the opportunity to quietly disappear; for all his bulk, he hadn't really been looking forward to the inevitable interview with the Boxingdale launch manager.

I suppose the most surprising thing about the entire event was that nobody was hurt, no-one even got wet. *Pride of Raasay* was eventually salvaged, patched up, re-engined and made seaworthy in time for the following season. Her new skipper was a much quieter individual altogether, and she was now no longer the instrument of terror upon the lake which she had once been.

As for Boxer, there was a rumour that he had emigrated to Patagonia and was busy teaching the natives how to distil potato wine.

CHAPTER 4. *Merganser*, and Other Boats

THAT first wonderful season on Birblemere drew to a close all too soon and holiday time was over. I went back to London, where I was lucky enough to land a job which I held right throughout the following year. The capital at that time was approaching the height of its fame in the 'swinging sixties'. The sheer size of the place oppressed me now that I had become used to a tiny village like Bulswick. Occasionally I would go out to a pub in the evening in order to talk to anyone who was willing to listen, and to drink a watery liquid which Londoners have the effrontery to call beer. So many people seemed to come from away that the usual opening remark would not be, "Hello, what do you do for a living?" but, "Hello, where are you from?" On one occasion I replied that I'd come down from the Lakes. "Oh yes," my new acquaintance said. "Where's that?" "Up north," I replied vaguely. "Oh yes," he said again, "I went to Birmingham once, is it anywhere near there?" I tried to explain that it was a bit farther up than that but he was not to be shaken in his belief that there were no roads north of Manchester. Somewhat hurt by this attitude, I informed him that dog sledges left every hour on the hour from Manchester so travelling was really quite easy.

If I wanted to be alone I would stay up all night and go for a walk at four or five o'clock in the morning through Chelsea and down to the Thames to watch the tugs and lighters feeling their way cautiously down the river. I would contemplate the water drifting slowly by as the great river rolled to the sea, or perhaps stroll along towards Westminster and pause on the bridge to gaze at Big Ben and the Houses of Parliament. Wordsworth, standing on that very spot, might indeed have thought earth had not anything to show more fair - but could he really have forgotten Grasmere? I certainly hadn't. At any rate, as the days lightened at the end of that second winter I began to think more and more of Birblemere, yearning for the fresh air, the soft outlines of the fells, the clear water, the tumbling becks, the silent woods.... until eventually I could stand it no more.

I telephoned the firm from London. Captain Wright answered. "Hello, it's me - Brian - here. Are there any jobs going this summer?"

"Start on the 19th," he replied, and put the phone down.

I went away cheered by the familiar reticence of Bulswick & Lake Launch Services, to spend the next few days trying to work out which 19th he meant - March, April, perhaps even May?

I arrived back in Bulswick a week before Easter and was immediately glad to be breathing clean air again. Back on the beach there were no big hello's or, "What have you been doing this time?" All I got when I started work was "Morning", as though I'd never left. Life ticks along so slowly in this part of the world. Several boatmen asked me if I were ill because I was very pale through working indoors.

While I was away a brand new launch had arrived, and I found her waiting at the pier dwarfing all the other craft. She was all glass - shiny and gleaming, a very racy appearance. Even the fleet flagship *Mallard* looked shabby beside her, but David didn't bother since he'd now been promoted captain of the new vessel. *Merganser* was her name, and she resembled a floating greenhouse. Many of the passengers mistook her for a hovercraft or a hydrofoil, and some of them continued to think so even after they'd been out on her.

It marked the slow dawning of a new era on Birblemere. The firm, which had previously been run in a rather carefree, amateurish fashion, slowly started to sharpen up - to become more efficient, more professional. It was so slow a process as to become almost unnoticeable, but looking back over the last twenty or thirty years from my vantage point in the present, there is a big difference. One thing, however, hasn't changed and I hope never will: we still make mistakes and get into foolish situations. But what would life be without a little comedy from time to time?

Merganser with her novel lines attracted a great deal of attention and became a very popular craft: she was the first 'waterbus' as they called this new type of vessel, and pointed the way to the shape of things to come. She was the forerunner, first in a line which was to stretch ultimately to the mighty *Lakeland Rose*, the launch of the future, replacing most of the traditional wooden launches which had plied on Birblemere almost since the beginning of time. Incidentally *Merganser* proved the old men wrong when they shook their heads pessimistically and said that fibreglass would never last.

Like David, I too had been promoted that season. My new command was *Gannet*, a bigger and faster launch than my little *Shelduck*. *Gannet* had to be properly looked after since for some reason she was a special favourite of Captain Wright - perhaps he'd driven her himself as a young man.

I was pumping her bilges out one morning (that was her only drawback - *Gannet* leaked like a sieve) when a youth came and sat down beside me, introducing himself as Cecil. He was a new boy, as I had once been, and had just completed a couple of terms at theological college - this was a vacation job for him. I'd never met an apprentice vicar before so I was interested in what he had to say for himself.

Cecil was an earnest and not unintelligent young man, and tried very hard to grasp the rudiments of boat-handling, but with a marked lack of success. Just as some people cannot drive a car, there are some who can never master a boat. Cecil was one. He would drive back and forth in the bay using the same stretch of water all the time, wearing his gearbox out and getting nowhere. The boat always "got the boss of him" as we say.

This was not altogether surprising as poor Cecil had been condemned to drive *Wizard*, and if ever a boat was feared and hated *Wizard* was that boat. All boats have their good and bad points - that's what gives them character - but *Wizard* had only bad points. As you boarded her the steps wobbled, almost pitching you onto the deck. If you recovered your balance and decided to go into the cabin you were almost certain to bang your head in the doorway, which looked deceptively high. Most of us learned to avoid that particular trap, but the passengers never did, and any who *did* manage to escape that hazard would then walk into a roof beam which projected a little lower than the others.

The driver had to sit (there being no room to stand) behind a small windscreen of perspex which was by now very old and scratched, effectively blocking out the sunlight but not the wind and rain which came in round the sides. You sat astride a large box with the wheel before you, a large gear lever to your right and a throttle to your left. Due to the position of the wheel it was impossible, unless you were built like an orang-utan, to reach both gear lever and throttle simultaneously.

Wizard had a petrol/paraffin engine which never ran out of surprises. She would refuse to start. She would start first time and then stop on the way round for no reason at all, always when you were surrounded by other craft or were too close to the shore. You had to start her again cursing under your breath while the passengers stared at you. *Wizard*'s favourite trick was to cut out when you came alongside and changed gear, just when you needed the reverse to stop. The luckless driver would be forced to jump for the pier, rope in hand, to take a few turns round the nearest post in order to stop the boat before she bumped into the one moored in front. Another alarming habit was for her to jump sideways just as you finished reversing - unless of course the driver allowed for that, in which case she wouldn't do it and thus leave an embarrassing stretch of water between the boat and the pier.

She was always unpredictable. Some boats, for instance, would do *this* when the wind came from one direction, or *that* when it blew from another; but *Wizard* never exhibited any pattern at all. You might for instance be cruising along dreaming of your favourite pin-up girl dancing a can-can in a grass skirt when without any warning the gear lever would leap out of gear and catch you an agonising blow on the patella. If you retaliated by angrily thrusting the lever forward again you'd trap your thumb between the end of the lever and the engine case. In fact the only thing that could be said in *Wizard*'s favour was that if you were not her driver you could almost guarantee a laugh at the expense of the luckless fellow who was, especially if she was coming in to land. To our great relief she was sold some years ago and went south. I often smile to myself and wonder what havoc the old *Wizard* must be causing on the Thames.

The time came inevitably when Cecil was judged fit enough to take his test; we waited all morning for his return. When he eventually arrived back, his face was ashen. Tom told us what had happened. At first all had gone well, *Wizard* had behaved perfectly when they landed at Mr Wall's pier. Tom and Mr Wall had sensibly decided to remain on the pier while Cecil was sent off on his own to show his paces. He managed to reverse through a maze of moorings and then come back in again but just as he was coming alongside *Wizard* started playing up and her engine stopped. There'd been a bit of a panic until the three of them managed to stop the boat manually, and Mr Wall unwisely asked Cecil to back out and come in again. This he did, but so unnerved was the poor lad by his first landing that he came in far too fast, the engine screaming, and at the vital moment panicked and instead of reversing shoved the gear lever forward again, shot past Tom and the Ranger and disappeared through the open door of the Ranger's boathouse. Seconds later there came a sickening crunch as *Wizard* rammed the Ranger's patrol boat right up the slipway and splintered the transom. The next minute Cecil came slowly and wretchedly out with bits of the Ranger's boat dropping off *Wizard*'s bows into the lake.

Nobody spoke. John Wall's new patrol boat had been his pride and joy. It had also cost the Birblemere Navigation Board a lot of money. Cecil, needless to say, failed his test - the first time this had happened in anyone's memory. In punishment Captain Wright sent him over to bail out the rowing boats. Cecil spent an entire season bailing out rowing boats, no doubt drawing on his theological studies for the necessary qualities of patience and humility.

The next aspiring driver handled his boat with such speed and panache that the Ranger sarcastically suggested he fit safety belts for his passengers in the case the boat should stop suddenly. His name was Duncan Preedie and he was an ex-submarine officer. We promptly renamed him Speedy. Speedy was assigned to *Suzanne*, a rounded, clinker-built launch which looked not unlike a tug. *Suzanne*'s peculiarity was that the wheel always pulled to port unless you held on like grim death, but Speedy overcame this impediment by devising a steering lock to keep her going in a straight line so that he could march up and down amongst his passengers puffing his pipe, and issuing brief commentaries between puffs. This steering device consisted of a series of elastic straps hooked to various projections on the control panel, and worked very well until some curious child unhooked a crucial end, whereupon the entire apparatus flew up in the air and disappeared over the side.

So thrilled was Speedy with actually being on the surface at last instead of under water (where he had never been able to see where he was going) and free from naval discipline that he went quite wild. One of his games was to race the old cable ferry which used to cross the lake not far from Boxingdale, seeing how close he could pass ahead or astern of it without being caught like a fish on a line. Old Fred Fogghorn the ferryman entered into the spirit of the thing and would try to catch him, but Speedy was too good for him.

Except just once, when he misjudged his distance (it was raining and the windscreen was all steamed up) and the ferry cable came up beneath *Suzanne*'s keel just as she was passing over, to catch fair and square on the large projecting nut where the rudder post fastens to the skeg, at the nethermost part of the keel. The boat stopped instantly, but Speedy didn't. He fell forward, banged his nose on the windscreen, lost his perch on the driver's stool and ended up in an undignified heap on the deck. The ferryman laughed all the way to the other side of the lake and back again.

Another of Speedy's games was to devise as many variations to the standard cruise as possible. Instead of simply circumnavigating the islands like everyone else he would double back on himself, go round a couple in a figure-of-eight so that when he emerged his passengers were completely disorientated.

Landings were his biggest challenge. Much to Captain Wright's chagrin *Suzanne* was often observed charging at the pier with her bows in the air and her stern digging deep into the water, trailing a huge cloud of exhaust smoke. Speedy used to land as fast as he dared and throw the boat into reverse at the very last minute, stopping only just in time. *Suzanne* had a very good reverse - she was one of the few boats whose propeller was designed with exactly the right pitch.

All very impressive until something goes wrong - as of course it did. *Suzanne* didn't take very kindly to this kind of treatment and one day showed her displeasure in a uniquely memorable way. Speedy came flying in as usual like an express train, the passengers' hair streaming in the wind, threw *Suzanne* into reverse as was his wont, when there was a sudden clank from beneath the boat as the propeller flew off. At that speed nothing could be done. Speedy just stood there at the wheel, his mouth wide open in horror as *Suzanne* bounced off the pier splintering woodwork as she went and charged up the shingle beach to finish just short of the bus stop, where she rested against the railings at an alarming angle.

Nobody had the wit to shout "Fares please!" but someone did suggest later that Speedy plant a few potatoes in the large furrow he had just ploughed. Captain Wright and the boatbuilders didn't see the funny side, but then they never did have a sense of humour. Duncan Preedie has the distinction of being the only launch driver on Birblemere to have unloaded his passengers down a ladder onto dry land.

One of the oldest boatmen on the lake in those early days was a character named Lewis Killigrew. There was a certain nautical flavour about him, an air of salt and seaweed, and when I asked him if he'd ever been to sea he replied that he'd spent twenty years before the mast, and another twenty after it had been invented. That was as much sense as I ever got from him, for as I remarked earlier, these boatmen were in the main an uncommunicative lot - except for regular requests for food.

Lewis actually ate very well but always complained his wife didn't feed him. Clearly he felt it his duty to uphold the old boating tradition, for boatmen never refuse food or drink when offered. In fact if you leave a half-eaten pie lying about for five minutes it will be gone when you get back; we eat more bread than the ducks, and drink more tea than an entire Women's Institute. In his old age Lewis referred more and more frequently to his empty stomach, and this had a result which nobody could have foreseen.

An American couple who were staying at the exclusive Devonshire Hotel wandered down to the beach on their first day, and here they discovered Bill Birblethwaite. For a while he regaled them with his characteristic drivel but after a while he grew tired of their equally frivolous questions and used the time-honoured ploy of passing on one's problems to someone else. Therefore he pointed to Lewis who was slouched on a nearby bench, apparently sound asleep, and said to the couple, "Why don't you go and have a word with that old seadog, he knows far more about the lake than I do."

The American couple went over to Lewis. "Hi there," but Lewis didn't look up. "Say, something wrong, old man?" asked Sir.

"I haven't eaten in three days," said Lewis, clutching his stomach and staring dismally at the ground.

"Why, you poor old man," said Madam. "Come along, Elmer."

And off they went. Bill Birblethwaite smiled to himself because he'd overheard all this and thought it would be a good tale to tell in the club that night. But lo and behold, ten minutes later there appeared from the direction of the Devonshire Hotel a trio of immaculately clad waiters bearing trays, led by Madam. They converged on Lewis and placed the trays before him. One was laden with cold meats, potatoes and lots of other goodies, another contained a selection of sweets, while a third bore an ice-bucket containing a bottle of excellent table wine.

Completely taken aback, Lewis could only stammer: "Th.... thank you, dear lady. Thank you." Then he began to stuff the food into his mouth with the speed of a starving man, frightened lest she learn the truth and take it all away again. When several other boatmen, warned by Bill, began to drift toward this banquet - attracted as ever by the prospect of free food and drink - the lady shooed them away and began to upbraid them, telling them they were greedy pigs and ought to be ashamed for allowing the poor old seadog to get into such a state.

After that episode Lewis had a new respect for visitors from across the Atlantic. Until then, whenever his American passengers asked questions about the lake he had always muttered at them in the local dialect, of which they couldn't understand a word. A typical example of his communicativeness was a reply he once gave to a query about the martello tower[3] on Ross Holme: "Say, whaat's that caastle?"

With commendable nonchalance Lewis replied: "Dunno, 'twarn't theer yisterday."

---

[3] Not to be confused with Rosthwaite Keep (see p. 21)

CHAPTER 5. Meths Maloney, and Other Disasters

WHENEVER a stranger wanders in the direction of a group of boatmen one of them will say, "Look out, silly question time." Many a visitor, moved by the beauties of the surrounding landscape, will engage you in hours of conversation about Birblemere and district, how lovely it all is, where would you recommend us to go tomorrow, etc. etc. This is all very nice and can give you a feeling of pride, as if you had created the hills and lakes with your own hands - but we *do* have a job to do, and it can be difficult to break away from these good people without seeming rude. Amongst the hundreds and thousands of quite ordinary and innocuous remarks addressed to boatmen, or overheard by them, there are a number of highly ludicrous, indeed incredible questions, and no matter how long you have worked on the lake, every year you hear something new.

My first silly question took me entirely by surprise, and my lack of experience in handling such things led me to become involved in a pointless discussion which lasted the length of the cruise, at the end of which both the questioner and I were more baffled than when we had started.

"Do the islands float?" was the remark which started it. Package coach tours 'doing' Europe in an afternoon sometimes ask: "What lake are we on?" People frequently board the boat and ask, "Which is the front?" to which one replies with the smoothness of the music hall artist: "The sharp end," or even, "the bit that goes first." But I'd never heard of a floating island before. Rock Holme, for instance, was solid enough, as you'd soon find out if you took a launch within fifty yards of the place.

Captain Wright was often asked: "How long is it?" and purposely misunderstanding a simple enquiry as to how long the next cruise will take, sometimes replied, "About forty feet, madam." - ie. the length of the boat.

I was once asked: "When do we get to Bittermere?" - the passenger apparently believing that all the lakes are one vast sheet of water divided by invisible lines like county boundaries. On reversing away from the pier I have overheard: "Are we going backwards all the way?" Some other remarks are: "Is the lake tidal?" "Is it man-made?" "Is it salt or fresh water?" "Can I get a boat to Croswick Mere?" The answer to that was met with: "Why not?" prompting the reply: "Because the mountains play havoc with the propeller."

I once had to deal with: "The hills all look so smooth, do the farmers have to mow them?" And still on the subject of hills: "Are there any monasteries on top of the mountains?" (Perhaps confusing them with Monte Cassino). Back on the surface: "Are there any crocodiles in the lake?"

One delightful old lady had been the first person to board, and was discussing with her friend where would be the best place to sit. They chose to sit at the front, and after a minute or two she said to her friend: "We won't sit here, we'll be sitting over a wheel."

But I suppose the strangest question of all came when we were cruising along the well-wooded shoreline of Friars Fell. "Say, are there grizzlies in them woods?" from one of our transatlantic cousins.

But back to our boating adventures - or more correctly, misadventures. It was during my third (I think) season with the firm that an individual called Meths Maloney joined us. Meths was a powerfully-built eccentric in his early thirties, with flaming red hair to match his flaming temper. He wore horn-rimmed spectacles with beer-bottle-bottom glass in them, and on wet days when they misted up he would round on the nearest passenger and ask loudly (he said everything loudly): "Have we passed a red buoy yet?" I suppose this was a silly question in reverse, since we were passing red buoys all the time, and anyway how would a passenger know a red buoy if he saw one? "... I can't see a thing in here," Meths would continue. "Even on a fine day you need damned good eyesight to see through these things."

Meths Maloney drank, whenever and whatever he could. He had no sense of moderation and was highly delighted when called upon one afternoon to take a small party of Austrian naval gentlemen to Biskey Landing, stay for coffee, and then return. He maintained afterwards that these nine gentlemen comprised the entire Austrian navy and that their hands were calloused from all the rowing.

They all duly arrived at Biskey after an uneventful trip, but instead of taking them for coffee Meths led them into the nearest bar to sample the local real ale. By all accounts they did more than sample it, they almost drank the place dry, and Meths was unaware that the Austrians were adding all kinds of things to his drink behind his back. After numerous "Prosits!" or "Grüss Gotts!" or whatever they say in Austria, closing time drew near, and a courteous barman eventually managed to herd them through the door. Singing raucously, they weaved their way back to the boat only to find the driver had been left behind. Nothing daunted they went back to the pub to find Meths lying insensible on the floor of the gents. They managed to carry him down to the boat, deposited him on the deck in a crumpled heap, started the engine and tried to set off only to discover (after some time) that they were not moving because the boat was still tied to the pier. Then they cast off and made their erratic way back to Bulswick.

One might naturally expect them to miss the pier on arriving back, but they actually missed the *bay* on the first attempt and had to turn round and come back again. By this time we all realised that there was something wrong, the boat was clearly not under proper control and on her third pass those of us with binoculars could make out three passengers behind the wheel and no sign of the driver. So we made ready with boathooks, fenders and ropes and when the boat finally came close enough to catch hold of and pull into the pier, there was Meths lying on the deck semi-comatose and vomiting feebly into the bilges. Those Austrians hadn't enjoyed themselves so much in years, but an ambulance had to be called for the driver. They took him away, pumped his stomach out and kept him in overnight.

Meths was never a man to refuse a challenge. Glancing astern one day he happened to see Speedy rapidly catching him up, and his natural instinct was to open the throttle and make a race of it. Speedy was in *Suzanne*, and she could knock on a good few knots when occasion demanded, but Meths was in *Pegasus*, a diesel-engined launch which in those days was the fastest in the fleet. He had been put on a diesel boat because Captain Wright was worried that given a petrol-paraffin boat Meths might drink the paraffin. Fast as she was, *Pegasus* had a full complement and Speedy hardly any passengers, and since the weight of the cargo can noticeably affect a boat's performance, Speedy was gradually gaining on him. It was blowing a gale that day, both boats had the wind (and the waves) behind them, lifting them along.

There came a point when they reached a narrow channel between a couple of small islands, really only wide enough to take one boat at a time, and that had to stay in the middle. Speedy, however, was determined to overtake Meths, and Meths was equally determined to thwart him. They raced into the channel neck and neck, separated by only a few feet, a tidal wave of combined washes kicked up behind them, thoroughly enjoying themselves and oblivious to the feelings of their passengers.

Even so, they might have got away with it if, lo and behold! John Wall the Lake Ranger had not chosen that moment to come round the island from the opposite direction. He perceived the situation at a glance: two big, fast launches and a mountainous wash coming straight for him, realised that he had only a few seconds in which to react, panicked, threw the wheel hard-a-port and shot straight up the shore. The succeeding wash lifted him yet farther up the beach, and by the time everything had cleared and he was able to look round, both Speedy and Meths had vanished round another island.

On returning to Bulswick, Meths rather recklessly chose to shout across to one of his colleagues: "Hey, guess what! We've just left the Lake Ranger halfway up a tree on Thick Holme!"

Captain Wright overheard this remark and came marching down the pier demanding to know what had been going on. After hearing a very much diluted version of events by the culprits, who blamed the whole thing on a cabin cruiser from the local hire firm, Weekends Awash, he insisted that one of them - preferably Speedy - go back and tow the Ranger off again, and while he was there take the opportunity to apologise. Speedy duly set off at full speed in *Suzanne*, only to meet the Ranger being towed ingloriously back to port in Deansgate Wyke by a passing cruiser which had managed to pull him free.

"Are you alright?" yelled Speedy as *Suzanne* came within hailing range.

"No thanks to you," came John Wall's reply. "You'll be hearing more of this." And it took a deputation of Meths and Speedy, personally headed by Captain Wright himself, to go round to the Ranger's office on bended knee and humbly present their apologies, before that official could declare himself mollified. Speedy thereafter always maintained that the Ranger had brought the whole thing on himself for skulking behind the islands waiting to catch speedboats offending against the Navigation Rules, instead of patrolling in open water like a gentleman, where he could be seen.

Tobacco was one of Mr Maloney's phobias. He flew into a terrific rage whenever he was offered a cigarette (this happens quite frequently on boats) upbraiding the bewildered offerer with threats and even calling his parentage into question. Another pet phobia was cameras, which was unfortunate because there is *always* somebody pointing a camera at you. We boatmen must be the most photographed people in Britain next to the Beefeaters or the Life Guards. There is enough film exposed on Bulswick waterfront during the season to stretch right round the moon and back again. Gesticulating at the photographer with quivering, outstretched finger, Meths would roar:

"Don't you point that thing at me, sir!" And he would proceed to cover his face with his hand like Arabs do when a foreign tourist aims a camera at them, making a curious gesture which he said was to ward off the evil eye. Actually it bore a striking resemblance to Churchill's famous victory sign.

Meths Maloney has the dubious distinction of being the only driver ever to have broken four boats in one day. Number one was *Pegasus*, in which he commenced his morning cruise by reversing out, but unfortunately when he came to engage forward gear the gear lever came off in his hand, so he leapt on the bow waving it about and shouting until someone set off to tow him back in. The rescue boat, however, was not quite in time to prevent *Pegasus* drifting into a cabin cruiser that was being towed across the bay to the nearby boatyard, and succeeded in wrapping the tow rope round three boats.

Meths was next given a boat named *Skua* and sent on his way with the same load of passengers to try again. All went well until just as he was coming in to land the wheel fell off with a crash of chains and blocks, and there he was again standing on the bow and shouting, and this time waving the wheel about. As I towed him in I could see that the passengers were having grave doubts, they were probably very relieved the cruise was at an end.

Fortunately there were plenty of spare boats that day so Captain Wright sent him off on *Wizard* as a punishment, and it broke down behind one of the islands, where it was found drifting a couple of hours later, Meths having drawn attention to his plight by leaping about on the cabin roof, waving and shouting. Some of the people on a passing launch proceeded to take his photograph, perhaps thinking this was all part of the entertainment for the cruise.

When he had been towed in Captain Wright took it upon himself to give Meths a very severe talking-to, as if the whole series of calamities were Meths' fault, and then sent him off on another boat, *Gannet*, to the Oaktree Hotel to collect a coach party and convey them to Boxingdale. Actually they should have been collected half-an-hour ago, but Captain Wright had only just remembered about them, and Meths was the only driver he could spare. He was therefore told to get there as fast as he possibly could, but - Captain Wright could never make up his mind and always hedged his bets - not to thrash the engine or cause a big wash. Loosely interpreted this meant get there now, but don't get any complaints.

So Meths set off, employing the old boating technique used on such occasions which is simply, put everything forward and Trust In The Lord. On the way the engine began to overheat. Meths did not know about this - how could he, since he never bothered to look at things like temperature gauges? - until smoke started billowing out of the engine case. For although *Gannet* was a favoured boat, none of her gauges worked except the ammeter, and nobody ever looks at that anyway. Many of the gauges had been there since the days when *Gannet* was a steam launch, about fifty years ago. One of them still showed boiler pressure, and to start the engine you pressed a button marked 'Heater'.

Meths presently arrived off the Oaktree Hotel pier, which was crowded with people looking expectantly out to sea, with *Gannet* enveloped in a cloud of smoke and fumes reminiscent of a destroyer laying a smoke screen. Several gentlemen on the pier helped to put out the fire, getting very sooty in the process and then - rather surprisingly - the entire party boarded the boat and off they went on their cruise. They had to stop every so often for Meths to lower a bucket into the lake and dowse the smouldering engine case. When, due to the motion of the boat, the bucket was suddenly wrenched from his grasp to disappear forever into the murky depths, Meths had had enough. Perhaps he couldn't face Captain Wright yet again, perhaps he was sick of Birblemere and boating, perhaps he simply couldn't take any more - despite his appearance he was a sensitive individual - but anyway, he landed just short of Boxingdale, tied *Gannet* up securely, directed his party to the nearby coach park, then made his way back to his digs, packed his ancient motorbike and sidecar and telephoned his resignation later that evening from a hundred miles away. We all very much regretted Meths' departure for it had been most entertaining having him around. We were however running out of boats, so perhaps it was as well he left when he did.

CHAPTER 6. The CO2 Dance Ritual, and other Follies

MOST parties, of course, genuinely appreciate the time they've spent on the lake, but you can always get a minority who really are the limit. One such party that we've been taking regularly for years and years has been named the Beasts. They usually arrive in coaches round about lunch time and require to be transported to Boxingdale where their coach picks them up. Each person has been issued with a packed lunch and strenuously instructed by the coach driver NOT to eat it on the bus under any circumstances but to consume it on the launch. No sooner are they on board than they start various competitions amongst themselves, all based on the packed lunch. One group, for instance, will see how many screeching gulls each of them can attract to circle the boat and catch lumps of bread on the wing. Five minutes later the gulls send it all down again, dive-bombing the launch, the passengers and the driver with deadly accuracy.

Another group will be busy smearing sandwich fillings over the seats and windows to see who can cover the greatest area in the shortest possible time. And you wouldn't believe the quantity of orange peel that a skilled professional can cram into a tiny ashtray in the space of half an hour. I know because it takes just as long if not longer to prize it all out again. Half way through one season I got so fed up of doing this that I gave up in disgust and left the ashtrays to fester and ferment for the remainder of the year. Inevitably the time came when they had to be cleaned out - and it wasn't a pleasant task.

Some of the passengers - and you can actually hear them doing it - will place a banana skin on the deck, sometimes with the banana still inside it, and then proceed to rub their feet vigorously over it until it is reduced to a sticky, black, disgusting mess. Passengers with vacuum flasks open the windows and pour coffee all down the outside of the glass.

You may have guessed by now that there isn't a great deal of competition for the privilege of conveying these Beasts down the lake and you can always spot the unlucky chap who forgot to hide when they were due to arrive, and consequently had to take them. His boat is doing a straight line at full speed down the middle of Birblemere in order to arrive at its destination in the shortest possible time.

That is the first clue. The other is the dense cloud of seagulls circling over the launch until it has almost disappeared from view. You can just imagine the mess they are making over it, and over its passengers. Curiously, the passengers never seem to associate the act of feeding with the resulting deposits. In more recent years David Duckworth took to telling his passengers that seagulls were suspected AIDS carriers. That generally seemed to do the trick.

    Having been assaulted by the Beasts I try, if there's time, to calm my shattered nerves with some light physical exertion, namely by cleaning the boat inside and out. It needs a clean anyway - they always seem to manage to board the boat with one bagful of comestibles and leave four bagfuls behind.
    When the hull needs cleaning the normal practice is to board a rowing boat with a bucket of soapy water (Fairy Liquid works very well) and a lather brush, come alongside your launch and wash your way along the side. It is only then that you realise how big the thing actually is, and what a vast area there is to cover. I was once washing industriously away, watched by the usual disinterested crowd of shore-based admirers when another driver remarked that I was doing it all wrong. He was only new that year so I didn't take him seriously - I asked if he'd prefer me to dive underneath the boat and paint it with waterproof paint.
    This young man thereupon took it upon himself to jump down from the pier into the rowing boat and show me how it should be done. Unfortunately he hopelessly misjudged his leap - later maintaining that I'd moved the boat on purpose - missed it altogether and landed in the lake with an almighty splash and a yell of alarm. The watchers on the shore now proceeded to take a much more lively interest in the proceedings while Captain Wright, reacting very quickly to the situation (a drowned skipper is bad publicity) jumped onto the roof of *Crocus*, grabbed one of the old lead-weighted life rings kept there and threw it at the fellow struggling in the water. Luckily it missed him and plummeted straight down into the depths never to be seen again. This was not a very good advertisement for the quality of our life-saving equipment, but fortunately all the life rings have been replaced since then. The new driver managed to struggle out unaided; and this was how the Sub-Aqua Club was born.
    In order to join the Sub-Aqua Club, that exclusive coterie reserved for the elite amongst boatmen, it is first necessary to fall accidentally into the lake. The more amusing and dramatic your entry into the water, the higher up the social scale you will go. It is most important that this event be witnessed and if possible photographed by another boatman. It's no good doing as one applicant did, taking his coach party to a remote pier (Biskey Landing) and then stepping off it

backwards while waving goodbye to the departing coach. If we do not extract any fun out of the event the aspiring member must do it again. Most boatmen are members, and some of us renew our membership regularly. After all, it's pretty near impossible to spend your entire working life jumping into, out of and over boats without falling in the lake from time to time.

One member actually applied in his leisure time. He was enjoying some light refreshment at the Oaktree Hotel's whimsically named Acorn Bar one evening when someone came in to announce that a rowing boat had been discovered floating off the end of the hotel pier. Accompanied by a convivial crowd of companions he strolled down to investigate, beer glass in one hand and cigar in the other, and in the darkness walked right off the end of the pier. According to witnesses he surfaced still clutching his glass but minus his cigar; and he was swearing like a bargee. His exclamations of annoyance were so loud that he woke a lot of the hotel's guests, who all trooped out to see what was happening.

The blame for this event was ultimately laid at the door of a yachtsman who had moored his vessel for the night in an unusual manner: instead of tying up alongside the pier he had tied the bow to the very end so that the stern drifted right out into the lake. In the darkness one could be forgiven for assuming that the pier continued alongside the yacht, especially after consuming large quantities of the local brew.

The honorary (and perpetual) president of the Sub-Aqua Club is David Duckworth. His nomination and election proceeded unopposed after a memorable and spectacular performance in front of his colleagues. You will already have perceived that this situation contained all the key ingredients: his application was original, highly entertaining, and witnessed by other boatmen.

It was a pouring wet day in the late season, and poor David was wearing full washing-out gear (we called it our Number Two Dress Uniform) consisting of wellingtons, Hely Hansen jacket and trousers, sou'wester and rubber gloves. We were busy scrubbing out the engine compartment of one of the newer waterbuses, *Pandora*, which contained a pair of large CO_2 cylinders to be discharged in case of fire. One of these had been removed and placed on the pier for servicing. These heavy steel cylinders have a very sensitive mechanism - you have to handle them with as much care as you might an unexploded bomb - and unfortunately someone moved inadvertently and triggered it. David was standing nearby on *Pandora*'s deck when suddenly there was a loud 'WHOOOSH!!!' and a cloud of steam appeared from nowhere. The next thing he knew there was a red, evil-looking, torpedo-shaped object flying out of the steam straight for him and headed below the belt. Reacting with incredible speed he turned, leapt for the railings and vaulted up with the intention that the torpedo pass harmlessly beneath him and into the lake. Unfortunately a combination of soapy gloves and excess enthusiasm sent him clean over the rail to execute a magnificent one-and-a-half somersaults culminating in a perfect swallow dive - not an easy feat when you're clad in a full set of waterproofs.

Once in the water David prudently hesitated before surfacing. What if this evil object, now ricocheting about on the deck of *Pandora* like a thing possessed, were to follow him into the lake? After all, it clearly had his name on it. Shortage of breath, however, eventually brought him to the surface, where he might reasonably expect to find pairs of willing hands eager to assist him out of his dilemma. Not a bit of it. There wasn't a soul in sight so he struck out for the shore at a leisurely breast stroke. When he was halfway there Tom appeared, clambering along the side of *Pandora* towards him; David rolled over onto his back to see what assistance was intended.

None. They stared at each other for a while until Tom said eventually (he was always a man of few words): "Carry on then," so David did, demonstrating his back stroke by way of a change. By this time we had all gathered on the pier, grinning from ear to ear. Somebody lowered a life ring into the water, but he only did this because he'd just washed it and wanted to rinse the soap off. Soapy water dripped into David's eyes and the thing would probably have sunk him if he had not raised a protective arm. It was not until the poor fellow had reached the shore and staggered dripping from the lake that we all erupted into roars of laughter. We made so much noise that Captain Wright ventured out of his office to see what all the noise was about. He reprimanded David for playing about in the firm's time and then went back in again. So let that be a lesson to us all.

The cylinder of CO_2 had in fact behaved in exactly the same way as a balloon does when you blow it up and let go. The fiendish thing flew about on *Pandora*'s stern deck like a thing possessed, ricocheting port, starboard, forward and aft to finally plummet down the open hatchway of the engine compartment where it smashed in the cylinder head. David, subsequently inspecting the damage, was very thankful he'd moved when he did.

A couple of days later he was surprised to read the following communication which had been affixed to the door of his boat:

"Sterling Fire Extinguishers Ltd,
Pudding Lane,
London, EC1.

"Sir,
My attention has been drawn to an article recently published in the 'Morris Dancers and Maypole Frolickers Gazette' referring to an alleged solo performance by yourself which they describe as the Birblemere Reel. If I may quote:

"'A spirited and spontaneous dance using no more than a single fire extinguisher as a prop and the limited deck space of a Class V Passenger Launch was performed by David Duckworth with the wild abandon one associates with the fertility dance of the Bessarabian peasant..... dressed appropriately in local char fisherman's garb complete with 18th century charcoal burner's hat..... a delightful interpretation of classical ballet coupled with the agility and fleetness of foot of the picador, the double backward somersault into the lake and final languid swim to the shore brought a standing ovation from those fortunate enough to be present..... must surely rival the local rush-bearing ceremony as a standard tourist attraction.....'

"My board of directors and I feel that CO_2-jumping has a great future and are anxious to sponsor any future performance. We would envisage chartering a Sealink ferry to allow for onlooker participation. The Tourist Board are very keen to back the venture, which could perhaps be combined with an on-going plastic dry-stone walling competition.

"We look forward to your early reply, confident that you will go down with a big splash!
Yours sincerely,
Stanley Kettledrum
(Sales Director)"

There was the danger of the whole Sub-Aqua Club business getting out of hand as people attempted to better their fellows. Falling in today, however, merely entails the routine photographing of the event while the luckless boatman is floundering about, with a notice subsequently posted on the office notice-board.

The notice varies in detail but its content usually informs the applicant that if he feels he *must* go swimming fully clothed he should indulge his fantasy on his day off, not when he should be working; it is usually on the board by the time the applicant has emerged from the lake and dried off. Some drivers in a vain attempt to win fame for themselves even go in for repeat performances, the record so far being four applications in one season, including two in the same afternoon.

The position of photographer was held by the fleet chaplain Mr Charles Charcake (nephew of Claude, the Biskey Landing boatman with the artificial arm and the foul-mouthed jackdaw). We called him the Chaplain because of his habit of singing hymns to his passengers such as "Eternal Father, strong to save" over the tannoy. He was a boatman of many years' standing who always seemed to be standing at the right place at the right time (or at the wrong place at the wrong time depending on your point of view), smiling silently to himself and obviously enjoying every moment.

But now we come to *real* swimming. Every year swimmers arrive from all over the country to attempt the full length of Birblemere. Why they should wish to do such a thing quite defeats the imagination - perhaps, like Everest, because it is there - and of course they have to be accompanied in launches driven by us boatmen.

Long distance swimmers are big, hefty people covered in grease. Each one is accompanied by a rowing boat in order to steer him or her in the right direction since you can't see very well where you're going with your head partly submerged - and also to effect a rescue if necessary, as it very frequently is.

On the first such occasion on which I was to accompany the swimmers I was still driving *Shelduck*, my old favourite. By the time the first mile had been reached the race was spread out in a long line and the first casualty had occurred. A swimmer had got cramp and the man in the rowing boat was standing up frantically waving a flag. I waved back, but was told to get a move on and go to the rescue. So *Shelduck* screamed to a halt beside the swimmer and we all leaned over the side to grasp an arm or two, and pulled. In fact this turned out to be a well-built lady swimmer and I thought we had done very well to get her halfway up the side, but with all our weight on one side of the boat the swimmer was still in the water and we were pulling *Shelduck* further and further over, threatening to capsize the boat and make swimmers out of us all. We gave a determined heave and she slipped through our fingers like a cake of soap, absolutely covered head to toe in grease.

In desperation we tied a rope round her and towed her slowly alongside until we reached a shallow area of shore, where she lay beached like a stranded whale. Thereupon she was rubbed vigorously, given a cup of coffee from a thermos, and eventually circulation was restored. She thereupon stood up and pronounced herself fit and ready to carry on. But unfortunately she now came up against a far worse opponent than cold water: the Rules which govern amateur swimming. Because she had touched a boat she was automatically disqualified and had to retire. Rather tough on the poor lass, I thought.

By the halfway point the swim was spread out over three miles of lake. John Wall in his Lake Ranger's patrol boat was scooting up and down to keep inquisitive speedboats at bay, while a couple of hired launches patrolled slowly backwards and forwards carrying relatives and friends of the swimmers, and anyone else who might be interested.

The winner did it in under eight hours, quite impressive for the cold waters of Birblemere, but my admiration went out to the fellow who completed the course with a pair of artificial legs. Actually he didn't, he unstrapped them for the event and sent them on ahead by boat, saying they would only get in the way. He propelled his much reduced bulk using powerful arms and I thought the Rules might get him on that, but apparently not. The last swimmer in the line was retrieved by *Shelduck* shortly before dusk three miles short of the finish. He had been in the water for over ten hours and the poor fellow's skin was a bluish purple with cold. He had only given up because his limbs had refused to discharge their proper duties of propelling him through the water, and it took a full hour to thaw him out properly.

Falling in the lake, although cold and wet and undignified, is far more preferable to the experience undergone by a driver named Douglas MacBride. One of the most terrifying experiences a boatman can have is to be in danger of losing his boat when there are passengers on board. This unusual state of affairs can best be illustrated by recounting the Fall of MacBride. He was landing *Crocus* one day with a full complement of passengers, but due to a navigational error found that he needed to travel sideways towards the pier for a distance of four feet. This was impossible since boats are designed to travel forwards or backwards but not sideways, so there were two courses open to him: either to back out and start all over again, thereby drawing unwelcome attention to himself from his more experienced colleagues; or to jump for the pier holding a rope attached to the boat in order to pull it in, again hoping nobody would notice.

He chose the latter course and jumped. He only just made it as well, and was starting to reel his craft in like a fisherman landing a prize catch when he realised that the boat was moving backwards down the pier. To his horror he realised he had committed the cardinal sin of leaving the controls while the boat was still in gear. *Crocus* was in reverse and there wasn't a hope in hell of holding her, she was too powerful for that, and there was no convenient post round which to take a couple of turns with the rope. He was now walking back down the pier clinging to the end of the rope as the launch receded into the open lake, rapidly coming to the end of his tether.

Douglas conceived with remarkable clarity a vision of the launch reversing out into a crowded bay with fifty passengers on board and no driver. Uttering a wild Highland yell he made a desperate running dive off the pier, flew over the heads of the first three rows of passengers and crashed into the cabin doors. The doors however had never been built to withstand such treatment and disintegrated with a crash of splintering woodwork and the tinkle of broken glass. He landed at the feet of his passengers with a long tear in his jeans and blood oozing from his right buttock. This time he brought the boat alongside properly and the people disembarked muttering: "Thank you, nice cruise," while the poor fellow stood there and bled.

It was a peculiarity of Douglas's to wear a string vest that summer - all day and every day. Even on exceptionally hot days when we all went naked to the waist he would retain his vest, which was nothing more than a lot of holes tied together by string. This was because the sun had burned diamond shapes all over his torso; he was too embarrassed to abandon the garment, for he would have looked like a walking chicken mesh.

It was in that year I moved out of my aunt's establishment and took up residence in a small flat above a garage - nothing like a bit of independence! The garage stood next to a large house set in acres of dense woodland and was used not to stable a car, or even a horse, but a donkey, and the donkey's name was Henry. Henry was a loving, lonely creature who so enjoyed company that he dug a hole in my staircase which ran up the other side of his partition, and he would stick his head through onto the stairway and talk to me.

I grew very fond of Henry and always had a chat with him on my way up to the flat on returning from work. He once shoved his head into my pocket and ate half a pound of peppermint creams that I had purchased for my girl friend out of my meagre wages - a small investment which I hoped would yield, in the fulness of time, a substantial dividend. But Henry was so affectionate I forgave him even that, and every pay day thereafter bought him a bag of peppermint creams, of which he never grew tired.

Henry's only bad habit - and it was a very bad one indeed - was to bray every morning through the hole in the staircase at an incredible volume. The first time he did this I rushed down thinking he was being attacked, or had been stricken with a sudden pain, but it was just his way of saying "good morning". He was an early riser and for the first few mornings woke me up in panic with his atrocious noise at five am precisely, until eventually I became used to hearing a hundred hounds of hell swinging on rusty gates baying and howling simultaneously.

That July I decided to throw a party (for no particular reason) and duly invited everyone I could think of. The party progressed as parties usually do until some fool went below and let Henry out. This was not a very wise thing to do. Henry went trotting off into the woods and then remembered that he was afraid of being out by himself in the dark and proceeded to panic, charging round braying horribly and bumping into trees and things. Everyone went out to join in the search for the errant donkey, but I stayed behind to search for some peppermint creams.

While all this was going on Douglas MacBride was engaged in entertaining a young lady of his acquaintance in the front garden. At this point the owner of the house, my landlord, alerted by a phone call from a neighbour complaining about the noise both from the donkey and from the party, drove up and parked with his headlights full on the lawn.

Illuminated in the glare of the headlights was a fellow wearing only a string vest who was apparently engaged in a wrestling match with a girl who was wearing nothing at all. Being an excitable sort of person the owner jumped out of his car with a howl of rage while his two pet, and equally excitable, Alsatians which he had brought with him jumped out barking loudly. Henry answered from the woods, MacBride twisted round to see what was happening, saw a pair of dogs bounding towards him, hopped rapidly across the lawn pulling his jeans up as he went and then legged it into the undergrowth pursued by dogs and owner who thought they were after burglars. There must have been at least thirty people blundering about out there, judging from the noise I could hear from the shadows to which I had discreetly retired.

Henry came back when he caught the scent of the peppermint creams I was wafting about, and he and I went back into the garage to eat them in peace whilst the uproar outside slowly subsided and eventually died away altogether as the guests drifted slowly home. Nobody came back to the party, but some of them told me later they had made their way home out of the wood by different routes, pursued by a strange gentleman who said he was looking for a couple of Alsatians.

For the next week or two that same gentleman was to be seen prowling around Bulswick in search of a young man wearing a string vest, which explains why Douglas had to sweat in a pullover all the time despite the prevailing heatwave.

CHAPTER 7. Washing Out, or Washed Out

THE boatman's aim is to provide a moving platform for visitors to admire the scenery in relative tranquillity. After all, that's what everyone comes to the Lakes for, and generally speaking that's what they find. We cruise gently along carving a furrow through those placid waters like a plough sailing over some broad field. We pass trees and woodlands of countless variety and colour, which on the slopes of Friars Fell are packed as densely as any tropical rainforest. When these have been passed the mountain peaks rise in the distance - not fierce and jagged like the Alps, but gentle and rounded yet still massive enough to command respect. A buzzard wheeling lazily overhead looks down on walkers who have paused for a picnic on the shore; the occasional angler mutely watches his line. All is peace and tranquillity.

We pass a brood of mallards paddling along in line ahead, they rise up and over the wash one at a time, their tiny webbed feet working furiously. A mute swan dips his long neck to forage for weed on the lake bed, then waggles his upraised bottom at us. Perhaps this one is from a brood raised last summer on Sedge Holme, and is now seeking a mate. Swans mate for life and generally keep to a chosen territory, so we get to know them well.

Perhaps the gentle drone of the engine, combined with the sun beaming in through the glass has lulled a few passengers into a light doze - although not the naturalist, whose keen eye has spotted a heron (or jimmy-crane as we call them) fishing from the shore in a pose of frozen immobility. Then at last we come gently in to rest beside the pier again, and the passengers yawn, stretch and smile, the cruise is over. They remark how peaceful the lake is, how lucky the driver is to have such an easy job, it's a job in a million, away from all the hustle and bustle of city life. When the lake is at its best it's easy to agree with them; but other times I don't.

There is another side to the coin. Life isn't always that easy. Take bank holidays, for instance - and we all wish you would, as far away as possible. We recall the sixth coach party of the day bellowing 'Cruising Down The River On a Sunday afternoon' (".... only it's Wednesday, tee hee hee!"), making up in volume for what it lacks in quality, and just as tuneless as the five preceding parties. And then there's the joker - there's ALWAYS one in every party - who shouts: "Ahoy there, when's the bar open?" or "Cast off forrard, cast off aft!" or "Now then, Captain Birdseye!" or "Is there a hole in the boat?" etc.

etc. And sure as anything when they get off someone will say, "Bet you never had a load like us before, eh?" and hit you on the back.

I smile wearily and the next party start filing on. "Ahoy there, captain! Will it sink? Ho! ho!" "Only once, sir," is the standard reply. Well, you have to say something or they take offence. Off we go again, fighting through the packed masses of craft, struggling to get through without hitting or being hit by dinghies, rowing boats, self-drive boats, yachts, cruisers, rubber inflatables, lilo beds, jet skis, water skiers, water bikes, swimmers, divers - the lot.

All the time your ears are assaulted by assorted noises on board your craft: 'Cruising down the river'; Jack talking to Doris five seats away; the persistent screaming of a baby; small children running up and down the gangway yelling their heads off; parents yelling at their offspring.... the catalogue is endless.

And the struggle doesn't end when you've made it out onto the open lake, for the open lake is packed with half a dozen yacht races taking place simultaneously, there are power boats and water skiers tearing around at full belt, and even the occasional parachutist being towed behind a speedboat. And these latter don't have it all to themselves either - half the time they're ducking and weaving out of the way of RAF jets whose pilots think Birblemere is good practice for a low level attack down the Volga. They're all having a whale of a time and are quite oblivious to anyone else. The fishermen have given up in disgust and gone home because the lake has been robbed of its tranquillity and turned into Piccadilly Circus in the rush hour.

Then there's always the child who's seemingly determined to fall overboard. He will pivot on his tummy over the guard rail trying to touch the water which is always tantalisingly out of reach, or stand up on the seats or on the boarding steps, all dangerous activities which have to be dealt with tactfully. The way some people behave you'd think they were here on holiday, out to enjoy themselves!

So you have one eye on where you're going, one eye on what is coming up behind you, 360° of the compass to watch, another eye on the control gauges and one more on your passengers. You get a persistent headache from the noise and try deep breathing exercises to still your shaking hands. You come through the fairway rubbing your tired, reddened eyes, past Shuttleworth Nab and back into the bay where, horror of horrors, the boats are so tightly packed you could almost walk across them to the shore. Fighting back a cowardly desire to turn round and go back to the relative peace of the open lake you manage to side-step through them all without hitting one, looking forward to a well-earned cuppa at Dora's café before going out again, but no - every launch is going out as fast as they can load, there isn't even time to go for a pee, the jetties are jammed with people, there's a queue fifty yards long stretching right back to the road, the waterfront is a seething mass of humanity. It's like Dunkirk all over again: they're practically wading out to meet you.

It's even busy on a wet Bank Holiday. All the boats go out with a cabin choked full of passengers, no-one sits outside, so your windows are misted up and you're doing just as many cruises except that you carry fewer people. There are nasty wet days when the management are not best pleased and we know that at night there will be gloom in the counting house. Sometimes on a busy day it may just happen that there is a dead boat - ie. a boat without a driver, who has gone sick or just failed to turn up for one reason or another. And then woe betide any ex-boatman unwary enough to be seen passing the beach for he will be pressed into service and unceremoniously hustled onto the spare boat, his protests ignored, for hay must be made while the sun shines; wives and girl-friends take second place. Do not imagine either that affecting a limp will exempt you, for it has been tried and found not to work.

> "When bank holidays are over
> No more sailing round for me;
> When it's back to washing-out
> Oh how happy I will be.
>
> No more pointless silly questions,
> No more dodging little boats,
> No more nerve-destroying cruises,
> I'll be placid when afloat.
>
> But in the depths of winter
> With the puddles round my knee,
> I'll look forward to Good Friday -
> No more winter work for me!"

The ancient and honourable ritual of washing out rowing boats takes place every autumn, or 'back-end'. As the season declines and the days grow shorter we reluctantly set up a pair of wooden trestles and assemble the tools of the trade: lather brush, wire wool, clumps of stiff bristles, several bars of soap in a large tin, and a prodder. This last is an instrument for removing small stones wedged beneath timbers. Everyone has his own favourite prodder:

some use an adapted wire coat hanger, others favour a penknife with one of those gadgets for taking boy scouts out of horses' hooves. You also need a bucket of clean water and a sponge for rinsing off.

Having secured for yourself the smallest and cleanest-looking boat on the beach you then proceed to strip it, removing the oars, flooring, seats, metal railings, etc. and put them in a neat pile to one side, hoping someone else will wash them for you. You then begin on the boat itself. Start on the inside, at the bow. First lather a section of woodwork to get it all nice and soapy, then rub it down with some wire wool rolled into a tight ball. You have to rub hard enough to remove the top layer of varnish, leaving the surface matt or dull and the copper rivets gleaming. Any tell-tale shine not removed will show up when the wood dries, leaving you open to the derisive comments of your eagle-eyed fellows. In order not to expend an ounce more effort than absolutely necessary I developed my own 'Beaufort' scale of rubs: five rubs per section of plank at force four, seven at force two, and so on. When you've rubbed down one section you take your clump of stiff bristles and vigorously poke them along the seams, under the timbers (or ribs) and then rinse it all off with clean water. The section should now be as clean as mother's washing and you move on to the next, and then the next, and so on until the entire boat is done, inside and out.

Sometimes two of you are working on the same boat, taking a side each, and then it becomes more interesting because you can race each other, seeing who gets to the end first. I've raced many a new washer and practically left them standing, but nobody could ever beat David Duckworth who could whistle through one side of a six-seater rowing boat in under half an hour and not leave a single plank unrubbed, every copper rivet gleaming bright as if it had just been newly hammered. He worked so fast because he'd been washing boats every back-end since the age of seven, and in those days boatmen were paid on piece rates.

When we've finished the rowing boats we start on the launches, which are slightly more complicated. When you think that there are approximately one hundred different bits to come out of each launch to be a washed and taken away to the boat sheds you'll begin to understand why it takes until December to get them all finished. To wash one rowing boat properly with all its fittings takes one man one day, and although some claim to do it faster there is always an argument concerning the thoroughness of their operations. One lovely morning in late October when Birblemere was flat calm, reflecting the thousand different hues of the dying leaves and we were all busy scrubbing away at a beachful of rowing boats, a lady came up and asked a perspiring boatman: "Do you do this every morning before hiring them out?"

One autumn it poured down, absolutely poured day after day without stopping. It was the wettest autumn on record. Well you've got to have the rain to keep the lakes topped up, but this was just ridiculous: nature had simply forgotten to switch the tap off. The waters of Birblemere rose higher and higher. The low piers from which the rowing boats operated were the first to disappear, followed by the self-drive piers and finally the launch piers. In the end all the launches ended up moored *above* the piers with lines disappearing from their sides into the lake - proving rather inconvenient if you wanted to take one away into the boathouse. The lake was so high all we had to do was open the doors (which took some amount of time since the water came halfway up them) and drive the boat inside - no need to bother with bogies or winching.

Some launches were reluctant to start, having been out of use for a month, and in any case were full of water. One boat in particular, the *Happy Wanderer*, took even longer than usual. She was an elderly vessel with a remarkable three-cylinder diesel which was even more elderly and the front of her engine case was occupied by a gigantic fly-wheel. To coax her into life you had to press the starter.... and keep pressing it as the engine made a continuous oing, oing, oing noise as it struggled to turn the fly-wheel. After half a minute or so of this the oings became faster and broke into a bub bub bum, bub bub bum, these sounds increasing in frequency and volume until the entire boat was vibrating like a demented drill and passengers' false teeth were dropping onto the deck. And then with a roar she was off! There was a great belch of acrid black smoke from her exhaust which usually drifted into the cabin and set everyone coughing and spluttering.

Happy Wanderer on this occasion had not been pumped out for some time, and when the fly-wheel started turning ("round and round went that ruddy great wheel", as the song goes) it picked up the excess water from the bilges to send two tremendous jets of mixed rainwater and engine oil up into the air before falling back to the deck and drenching David Duckworth who was trying to start her. It all looked very impressive and lasted until David, conscious of his exalted position as the Chairman's son and heir, had finally managed to move *Happy Wanderer* round to the boathouse. From his muttered comments it was clear he did not share our sense of humour.

The lake now extended right up and over the beach to lap

gently at the promenade, where Dora's café was six inches deep in water, and both the bus stop and the telephone kiosk were inaccessible to people not wearing waders. The little wooden shack which functioned as a general headquarters for Bulswick & Lake Launch Services was flooded to a depth of four feet. When the phone rang someone had to launch a rowing boat from up near the road, row twenty yards to the doorway, somehow wedge the bows inside and holding an oar in one hand answer the phone with the other, assuming the caller had not given up by then, as they usually had. One such call was from the Strickland Times, our local rag, asking if the lake had risen very high. Captain Wright, who had answered it, was not very amused and intimated as much to the caller; half an hour later a photographer arrived and snapped Captain Wright answering another call from his rowing boat, and the resulting picture was prominently displayed in the paper's next edition. A visiting tourist who had witnessed the whole complicated performance told us we should have built our office farther up out of the lake. No-one was inclined to disagree with him.

Leaping into a rowing boat in order to answer the telephone was not something which bothered old Bill Birblethwaite. He considered them new-fangled devices designed to confuse people - he always liked to see who he was talking to. He was once seen, when he thought no-one was watching, to lift up the receiver and gingerly put it to his ear. When the operator asked him what number he wanted he promptly dropped the thing on the floor and left the hut in a hurry, shaking his head in amazement and shock.

Some years ago fifty-pence pieces were introduced. This threw Bill completely, and he refused point blank to accept them. If you remember, this was just before we changed over from good old pounds, shillings and pence to our new-fangled decimal coinage. Old Bill was having none of it. On first being presented with a 50p. coin he looked at it in disgust, rubbed it, scratched it, held it up to the light, decided it was "furrin money" and threw it into the lake, to the astonishment of the customer and the fury of Captain Wright. Old, torn, greasy ten shilling notes were the only kind of money he would accept, and eventually the firm's losses through coins ending up in the lake were so great they had to take Bill's ticket machine from him and demote him to looking after the rowing boats. When in later years they deepened the water round the jetties to accommodate the larger, modern waterbuses, everyone crowded round the huge lump of clay and mud which the JCB had dredged up, grovelling on their hands and knees for the 50p's which old Bill had flung away. I hope they gave him a few, for old times' sake.

Poor old Bill - he'd had some rough customers in his young day, as he never tired of telling us. One event in particular which always comes to mind on busy Sunday afternoons concerns the time when Bill was sent out on *Suzanne* (that's the one Duncan Preedie ran up the beach) with a party of truly formidable females. It was a Lancashire mill outing, and having previously fortified themselves with several quarts of ale this band of harpies decided, at the insistent urging of their coach driver, to go for a cruise. Bill was the unlucky fellow who drew the short straw.

He was away for the entire afternoon. No-one knew what had happened to him, no-one had even seen the boat, and they started wondering if *Suzanne* had gone down; but when the boat hove in sight in the late afternoon, hours overdue, the terrified driver could be seen standing on the cabin roof minus his trousers and keeping a horde of women away with a mop. One of these was wearing Bill's peaked cap and had taken over the wheel. All the other boatmen laughed themselves silly, and when *Suzanne* eventually arrived back at the pier and the band of harpies had departed, a white-faced and still trembling Bill related that he'd been threatened with mass rape - or a ducking in the lake if he wouldn't consent. They'd partly succeeded in the first objective, if not in the second. He said later he'd go back to the trenches any time rather than take that lot out again.

Those were the days! But if, years ago, launches took the rough end of the trade, rowing boat customers were far more gentlemanly and refined. Gentlemen and their ladies would stroll along the waterfront after dinner and, if the evening were fine, would hire a rowing boat. The boats were immaculate - cleaned and polished, proper oars, rudders, a cushion on every seat, carpets on the floor, everything made to measure. But times began to change. Carpets disappeared first - they could never withstand the onslaught of the booted masses. Then the cushions went, mainly because they usually ended up in the lake. Finally rudders were phased out because they served mainly to confuse the customers, sending them round in circles.

Without rudders, boats are still out of control, but to a lesser degree. Yet some people still manage to row backwards round the lake for a full hour, very slowly and very painfully and quite oblivious to all the other boats being rowed the right way round. Some of them, again, sit in the boat facing the wrong way and then try to row with their arms behind their backs, which must be at least as painful as the medieval torture of the estrapade. A few of them are quite unable to grasp the principle of rowing at all, pulling the oars through the water in the traditional manner but then pushing them back again without lifting the blades clear. This results in the oarsman stirring up the water very impressively but not actually getting anywhere.

It's also very amusing to watch young men, out to impress their girl friends, striding along the beach in a manly, purposeful manner to demand a boat in a deep voice. All very masterly and the girls are suitably impressed until the he-men step into a boat and realise, too late, that they are now in a situation which is totally new to them. If you don't walk straight down the centre the little craft will start wobbling alarmingly from side to side, the newcomer loses his balance and ends up on the floor tripping over a thwart (seat to you) on the way and bruising his arms on the oars.

The oars get heavier, shorter, and thinner bladed each year: the object being both to slow the boats down and to eliminate the constant stream of breakages. At this rate we will end up with two very heavy stumps and no blades at all. One of our boatbuilders is currently working to develop an oar with rubber blades which will flex under a given pressure, allowing the oarsman to wear himself out rowing like fury but only propelling the boat along very slowly. Another experimental project involves a length of elastic fixed to the stern of each boat: as long as the oarsman keeps rowing he stays out but as soon as he tires he comes back in again, or if his hour is up he can be reeled in. That would save having to go out searching for lost boats abandoned by people who can't be bothered rowing all the way back to Bulswick.

"Come in, number six, your time is up - oh dear, it's number nine in difficulties."

Another idea was to build a huge rowing machine on the shore and dispense with the lake altogether. This would be a circular affair like a roundabout set in the middle of a paddling pool; customers would put their money in the slot and row round in circles for an hour or so. To simulate conditions out on the lake you could have a wave machine to make waves, a giant fan to simulate a gale, and boatmen throwing buckets of water over the customers to simulate spray. You would of course have to tip them for this privilege.

CHAPTER 8. Boating in Winter, or Lost in the Mist

IT wasn't until after three or four years of seasonal employment that the management of Bulswick & Lake Launch Services decided, out of the goodness of their hearts, to admit me to that select band of men whose services were retained right through the year, summer and winter. As will be shown, this is a somewhat dubious privilege. At first I was introduced to the washing out ceremony whose rituals have already been described; and such a wet existence did I come to lead that by December when all the boats had finally been put away I was growing webs between my toes.

Never in my admittedly limited experience had I known a firm that was so spread out as this one. During the winter the launches were kept in boathouses dotted all the way around Birblemere, not more than three in any one place. The self-drives and rowing boats were kept in all sorts of unlikely places in addition to the upper storeys of the boathouses. There were rowing boats in peoples' garages, in garden sheds, rowing boats in farmyards amongst the cows and chickens, in remote barns halfway up a fellside, on camping sites, and generally everywhere where you would *last* think of looking for a boat. All the boat fittings showed a similar distribution, and not necessarily going with the boat to which they belonged. Take footsticks for instance: the bits of wood you stick in notches set into the floor of a boat to push against with your feet as you row - I'll never forget the day when I was driven halfway up a mountain to just below the snowline where there stood an ancient stone barn miles from anywhere. "This," I was proudly told, "is where we keep our footsticks."

I'd no idea the firm possessed so many boats, they didn't seem to be all that noticeable when they were on the beach. So if, gentle reader, one winter you should stumble across a couple of rowing boats at the back of a shop or in a forgotten cellar, don't think they are lost; they are only waiting to be done up. Do not simply pass them by, dust them off and give them a coat of varnish; or to paraphrase the epitaph at Thermopylae:

"*Go and tell the boatmen, thou who passest by,*
That here waiting for a coat of paint we lie."

I have often wondered, but never sought to find out, whether the owners of these remote hidey-holes have consented to our using them or even if they know about it. They are the sort of unfrequented spots sought after by moonshiners.... now *there's* a thought.

A very frequent remark in the summer (we hear it several times a day) runs along the following lines: "Grand job you lads 've got there, what do you do in the winter, go to the Bahamas?"

We do NOT go to the Bahamas, we go to a little place in the Lake District which usually involves a muddy trudge through rain, hail, sleet or snow, and there we varnish our boats. They say that if you can see the fells in winter it means it's going to rain, and if you can't see them it *is* raining.

Doing a boat up is, in its way, just as meticulous a process as washing out. Each fitting from the boat, each item of equipment, as well as every square inch of the boat itself, must be rubbed down with sandpaper, dusted off, wiped down and a touch of varnish applied to the bare spots. The next day when the touching-up (this has nothing to do with sex, so calm down) is dry you touch it up again, and so on until you have three or four coats of varnish on the bare bits. Then you can rub it all down again, dust and clean it and give the entire varnished area of the boat a full coat through. When all this has dried (which in winter may take some time) it will probably need yet another light rub down, clean off, and another coat through.

Runs, drips, splashes etc. in paint or varnishwork are not advised as other boatmen will come a-visiting with the intention of spying these lapses out and gleefully bringing them to your attention. When first being taught to varnish I was advised to "*Put nowt on and spread it well out.*" This, apparently, was an aphorism of Chairman Duckworth.

Skilled jobs such as scraping a boat down to the bare wood and starting all over again are reserved for the more experienced boatmen. Varnishing cannot be undertaken in very damp weather so you have to pick your day with care or the dampness will ruin everything, leaving you with more work than you set out with.

The greater part of my first winter, however, was spent not in some draughty shed halfway up a mountain but in a freezing boathouse overlooking the quiet waters of Birblemere. The little skylight looking out over the lake gave a grandstand view of the changing seasons - as autumn became winter and winter, after a seeming endless succession of short and dismal days, gradually gave way to spring. Had my father, grandfather and even great-grandfather been boatmen they would have looked upon the same unchanging sight: the heavily wooded shore of Friars Fell now denuded of leaves, often glowing red in the dying rays of the afternoon sun, a deep carpet of brown leaves sometimes covered by a thin layer of snow, the rocks poking out blackly from beneath, while the distant fells would be capped in a mantle of white. In the foreground the lake was clear and still, the only movement being when, on occasional days of gale, the water would be whipped up into white horses outside the comparative shelter of the bay.

Often there were spells of fine weather in winter when the sun would shine all day from a crystal clear, blue sky to be replaced at night by an inky blackness ablaze with a thousand points of light. During such spells the frost would set in and quiet places like the bay at Bulswick would start to freeze over. I loved to watch the ducks trying to walk on the ice. Waddle, waddle, slip, QUACK! (in annoyance).

Flying in to land on the ice is the most difficult feat a duck can be asked to perform and is most amusing to watch. Landing is difficult enough as it is - soaring down, turn into the wind, bring the nose (or beak) up to stall, stop and alight all in one movement. They reach the stalling part alright but as soon as their feet touch the ice they lose control, their feet skid forward and the duck lands on his bottom. Alternatively their feet slip backwards and he slides along on his belly, very disgruntled, and often skates clean off the other side of the ice and into the water. Sometimes a forward skid can be corrected by breaking with his beak, digging it into the ice accidentally; then he struggles to his feet, snorting and puffing and shaking his feathers, looking round to see if anyone is watching. As with most creatures, ducks feel any loss of dignity quite acutely.

Ducks hang around the bay right through the year, living off the titbits people bring down to feed them. Mallards prevail, but we get occasional Aylesburys as well, or rather the curious hybrid which we've christened 'Maylesbury', easily distinguished by white feathers amongst the mallard brown. There was a duck one year that looked like a perfect Aylesbury, pure white, except that it was far too small and turned out to be of mixed parentage: all her offspring were white, except for one on which you could just detect a brown feather or two.

A few coots (actually we coined the plural 'ceet' by analogy with 'foot - feet') regularly join the mallards in the bay - they probably think they're ducks too. All the other makes of duck, like goldeneye or teal, keep to less populated parts of Birblemere.

At one time there was such a surfeit of ducks around Bulswick that some of them were driven right off the lake altogether. They took to crossing the busy road which skirts the bay (impeding all the traffic) to roost on the ornamental gardens. Then by degrees they took to waddling up the road into the village, invading the doorways of the many souvenir and trinket shops with which this part of Bulswick is infested in search of food. They even penetrated inland up the becks, invading people's garden ponds, roosting on their back lawns, and eventually founded an entire sub-colony on Birble Moss, high up on the fells two miles away from the lake.

Years ago (before my time, at any rate) anyone who fancied a duck for his dinner was allowed to go out onto the lake and bag as many as he wanted, so that ducks became a rare sight on Birblemere. Now no more. Duck-shooting was made illegal, they have bred and become fruitful and multiplied so that now the lake is thick with them, and occasionally they have to be thinned out. This is accomplished by luring a small flock together with handfuls of grain, firing a large net over them and capturing an entire, squarking vanload. They are then taken away to be released onto a remote lake or tarn, from which they will return even faster if their wings are not clipped. Clipped feathers will eventually grow again, but by then it is hoped that the ducks will have settled down in their new home and forgotten all about Birblemere.

At the beginning of March we have the annual pre-season panic. This involves rushing round getting the boats ready for launching so that the planks can swell up. In order for a boat to be ready, its fittings must first be found and then put in position. This is not as easy as it sounds. Every boat, without exception, has at least one fitting - a footstick perhaps, or a small piece of flooring - which can never be found in the general rush to get things moving again. It will usually turn up (unpainted) in a corner of a disused boatshed several weeks later, by which time a new one will have been made. Still to this day we have never found a foolproof method of ensuring that every little item removed from a boat when it is washed out will be there ready to put back the following spring. However carefully you store these bits away in October, however carefully they're numbered and filed, you can be sure that come March they'll have scattered themselves around half-a-dozen boathouses. I can remember spending one entire afternoon searching for the back-board of a four-seater rowing boat, only to discover that the boat never possessed one in the first place.

All the launches have to be complete for the Board of Trade inspection, which is of necessity very thorough. An inspector arrives in the autumn when the boats are pulled off, inspects them minutely and then writes down what repairs have to be carried out, and where. He then returns just before the boats are due to be launched in order to check that the work has been carried out satisfactorily, and then again once they are back on the lake to check that they are 'seaworthy' and that essential items of equipment are present and in working order.

Crocus, for instance, has to have four fire extinguishers (which are checked and tested independently), four buoyancy tanks capable of supporting X number of persons, life rings capable of supporting two persons each, a boathook, an anchor and cable, a bilge pump, a couple of buckets and a box containing sand. The box containing sand is meant to be used to smother small fires, but in these days of super-efficient fire extinguishers (remember the CO_2 Dance Ritual?) it would never even be considered. In any case it tends to become neglected - fires on board are after all such a rare event - and passengers drop cigarette ends, sweet wrappings etc. into it and if any of the sand is spilled the driver would probably top it up with a handful of pebbles from the beach.

Some sand boxes now contain only a handful of stones. If you had a fire there wouldn't be any point in throwing stones at it, although on the other hand it is always useful to have a supply handy to aim at speedboats coming dangerously close. I wondered once just how far the Board of Trade inspector would allow the deterioration of sand boxes to continue, so I tested it by removing the sand box from one of the launches and replacing it with a biscuit tin containing a couple of house bricks. At first he objected, but then saw the funny side. What he failed to realise was how rapidly equipment could be juggled about from boat to boat as soon as his back was turned. One year he certified the same boathook three times, and the same two buckets seven times.

No sooner is everything shipshape and Bristol fashion, every boat equipped with its statutory couple of buckets and box of sand, than Easter is upon us and off we go again. The bad pennies from last season or the season before turn up again from home or abroad, and set to with polish and window cleaners to make the fleet shine once more.

As soon as Easter and its early season hordes are out of the way, the new drivers start appearing and training sessions begin. If my services as an instructor are required, I sometimes recall that first lesson I had with Tom all those years ago. Things have changed a bit since then. Gone are the green-painted boatsheds whose doors I was so terrified of splintering if I failed to stop the boat in time; gone too are little launches like *Shelduck* and *Wizard*, and instead the new drivers have to train on boats such as *Mallard* or *Crocus*, which were once the pride of the fleet. Any newcomer is regarded with enormous interest as we old hands try to guess what manner of man this is and how much accidental fun he is going to afford us during his early days of driving.

The days following Easter are generally regarded by the boatmen as the best of the year. The early tourists have gone home, the rush is over for the moment and we can take it easy before summer properly begins. The days are lengthening rapidly, the sun is bright in the sky, the air starts to warm up, Friars Fell assumes a sprinkling of green, and the sound of birds is drowned by Captain Wright advertising cruises to a largely deserted waterfront: "Any more for a cruise, it's lovely on the lake."

The days begin with bright, frosty mornings, the thin mist is easily sucked off the water by the strengthening sun. There are spring flowers on the shore, hosts of golden daffodils adorning the lakeside residences of the rich, cherry blossom in May, more and more trees bursting into leaf until you can no longer see the contours of the land through them. Private houses which have stood out in the winter now disappear behind a mass of foliage, hiding away from the stares of the curious throughout the summer. A carpet of bluebells ripples in the woods. Long, quiet days arrive, plenty of time to keep the boats clean and the brasses polished, or you can listen to Bill Birblethwaite and his cronies with their tales of long ago; or you can listen to Captain Wright telling a new driver that it is time to depart on a cruise.

The obscure underarm gesture which had so baffled me when I first started driving had now disappeared, to be replaced by a verbal instruction. Various phrases were employed, such as: "Give it a roll of drums" or "Give it rhubarb" or (more obscurely) "Give it Wigan", from which one had to deduce, and deduce very quickly, that it was time to start up and cast off. These phrases were in turn replaced by "Ignite!" and then a month later by: "Throw some more wood on!" (from the days of steam). On hearing any of the above a new driver might not react immediately because he didn't understand the instruction, or whether it was indeed directed at him or at someone else, but he would not be left in any doubt for long because Captain Wright would bellow "THROW SOME MORE WOOD ON!" this time glaring at the driver concerned who would very quickly work it out and get away 'toot sweet' as they say across the Channel.

Captain Wright was a firm believer in the idea that if a person doesn't understand him the first time and then shouts the same thing at that person very loudly, then he will. Surprisingly, this often seems to work - especially with foreigners. For instance, if you request a party of Frenchmen or Italians not to stand on the seats in order to view the scenery/feed the seagulls/photograph each other they will just ignore you; but if you repeat the request at the top of your voice and in a rather more abrupt fashion, most of them will comply. Except, of course, the Japanese. Address the meekest of requests to a Japanese and you will be instantly and unquestioningly obeyed.

A more usual phrase to signal the start of a cruise is "Send it on!", which has endured for years. This strange shout galvanises everyone into action, but as often as not is followed by a long drawn-out "H-O-O-O-L-D!" as the ticket man spots a couple scurrying along the beach. Sometimes there can be as many as half a dozen "Send-it-on.... HOLD! Send-it-on... HOLD!"s before you finally get away. This has prompted disgruntled passengers to ask if we were working flexitime. After all, a late departure can unsettle them if they've been lured onto the boat with the promise that it will leave promptly.

We can go out and come back in again so many times that we end up feeling like yo-yos; and the "Hold!" always comes when you have pushed the boat too far out from the pier to be able to pull it back in again, and you teeter between ship and shore with the gap widening all the time, nearly fall in the lake, and end up jumping aboard and manoeuvring back to the pier with extreme difficulty. Sometimes the cry of "Hold!" will be taken up by other boatmen within earshot, and then by others farther away, the cry echoing round and round the lake front like the baying of wolves.

The air is crisp and clear, the sun shines down on distant fells that are often snow-topped, spring flowers around the shore hint that winter is over and summer is just round the corner. Very few boats are out on the lake besides ourselves, and there is an abundance of bird life on the lake, particularly the cormorants and shags who arrive in October in vast numbers and take over a number of small islands for the winter. One of their favourites is Rock Holme, the branches of whose trees are stained white and dying with the accumulated weight of guano. Many years ago cormorants were classed as vermin, and if you sent a pair of feet from any you had shot to the appropriate ministry (perhaps the Ministry of Deadlegs) the government would pay you sixpence. These birds soon realised their danger and left for more hospitable parts. On being informed that they are now a protected species they are back in force and ruining all our pretty islands.

Spring isn't all wine and roses. You can get cold, damp, rainy days when the only way to keep warm is to keep moving about - the sort of day when we all wish we were in the pub. There's only been one boatmen's local, all the years I've worked on Birblemere. This is the Black Cormorant, situated very conveniently within a hundred yards of the waterfront, but cunningly protected from a view over the lake by several other buildings placed in between. Very occasionally, on days when the weather was really miserable, some of us would sneak up around lunch time to the bar of the Black Cormorant, where we would sit round the log fire, drink the local bitter 'straight from the wood', and talk about boats or girls, as boatmen have always done since time immemorial. An old guide to the Lakes, written over two hundred years ago, mentions the

"... *little hamlet of Bulls Wick, where there is to be found a goodly Inn or Hostelrie at the sign of the* **Blake Shagge**. *Here you may perchance seek out a Boatman who will, for a Shilling, row you a short distance on the waters of Birble Mere, regaling you the while with tales of local lore, for it is said, every rock and bay hath its own Legend attached....*"

Boatmen are still doing the same thing some two hundred years later.

Occasionally in the spring there can be a fall of snow and instead of pumping the bilges out we have to shovel snow out of the boats. If it freezes during the night the ropes are as solid as steel hawsers and seem struck by a form of rigor mortis, retaining whatever shape or pattern they have been left in the previous day.

Days like that are bitterly cold on the lake, which is in any case ten degrees colder than the land. In these days of enclosed waterbuses that doesn't matter quite so much, but we all have memories of freezing feet and hands, watering eyes and frozen cheeks, the passengers huddled together in the cabin for warmth while we drivers stand outside lashed to wheel, facing the implacable elements alone.

It's amazing the weather in which people will pay to go for a cruise: howling gales, when they ought to be frightened out of their lives, pouring rain, when they won't see a thing except sodden foliage, or thick mist when they can't even see beyond the bows - it matters not, somebody, sooner or later, will ask for a cruise. I suppose that in such conditions if any customer can root us out of our hiding places, they deserve to be taken on the lake.

I remember one still, autumn morning when I was called upon to take a launch to the Oaktree Hotel to collect a Jolliways coach party, convey them to Bulswick where they would spend a morning browsing round the trinket shops, and then convey them all back again for lunch. Once I'd passed Shuttleworth Nab the fog clamped down like a blanket with visibility becoming less than fifty yards and the shore quickly disappearing from view. As I drifted on the mist grew thicker until I could only see a few feet of water ahead of the bows. In these conditions the Birblemere Pilotage Handbook tells you to slow down and sound your horn, whistle or siren at regular intervals. All very well, but the Rules don't tell you how to find your way and I felt a right twit sounding off my horn every minute or so with no-one around and no answering call coming back through the mist.

I was drifting alone in a lost world devoid of inhabitants. I thought I was on course, judging from the six feet of wash visible astern. Tom, in the past, had advised me that if ever I was out in the mist I should keep the wash in a straight line, and as he was a boatman of many years' experience I respected his advice. Ten minutes later a tree loomed out of the mist right in front of me, so I stopped just in time to prevent my bows running up the beach. I had made a landfall, but where was I? After all, most trees around the shores of Birblemere look pretty much the same. After a while I realised I had made the shore of Friars Fell, not far from Peartree Pier, which was not only two miles from where I wanted to be, but also on the other side of the lake as well. That meant I had described a vast semi-circle, completely missing two islands as I did so.

The realisation completely threw me, for a few minutes ago I had been quite certain of my whereabouts and now I was somewhere completely different. Making a rapid mental adjustment therefore I set off into the nothingness again, trying to correct the steering as I went and keeping a sharp lookout for red buoys, for the notorious Wreckrigg Rocks, very appropriately named, are not far from this part of the lake.

Twenty minutes later I made a perfect landfall at Peartree Pier. Off I went once more and back I came once more, drawn to the pier as if by invisible elastic bands. Three times in all I returned to Peartree Pier, or at least to the nearby tree, and heaven alone knows where I went in the twenty minutes or so between landfalls. I saw sign of neither buoy nor shallow, which one can hardly believe possible, knowing that part of Birblemere.

So I set off on my fourth attempt, this time trying really hard and concentrating, keeping as straight a line as humanly possible; after ten minutes I came to a red buoy. Keep it to port, another should appear in a minute, and lo! it did, so I knew then I was heading in the right direction. Seconds later the opposite shore came into view and I almost sailed up somebody's garden lawn, distances are so confusing in the mist. But now I knew where I was. Hugging the shore for the next mile or so I eventually felt my way alongside the pier of the Oaktree Hotel, and there was the party waiting patiently for me.

Of course I was almost an hour late, but they all seemed to think I was a genius possessed of a sixth sense to have been able to get there at all. I told them it took more than a bit of mist to keep us salty old shellbacks off the lake, and didn't mention my little diversion. By the time everyone had boarded and I had messed about in view of the shore the mist began to thin and the sun started filtering through. I delayed a while, ostensibly to enable the passengers to take photographs of a hazy sun piercing the mist, but really in order to gain time for the driver to collect himself and find his way back again.

Back at Shuttleworth Nab the mist drew aside quite suddenly as if a gigantic veil had been rent in twain, and I sailed into brilliant sunlight with a calm lake placidly reflecting a clear blue sky. The sight was so beautiful it brought a collective gasp of awe to the party of Jolliways travellers. Moments like this are worth six months of rain and gales.

It's a strange feeling being lost in the mist; as far as I know there is no way of beating it without mechanical aids, and radar sets were some way down in the management's list of priorities. Any noise gets bounced around in the fog and might be coming from anywhere. With nothing at all to guide you, you will always travel in a circle. I kept seeing what I thought was a faint outline of hills, just where they ought to be, but it turned out to be an illusion, a mist-borne mirage. One of the boatmen was once lost for an entire morning on the lake and eventually landed on an island only five minutes' journey from his starting point. To this day he has no idea of where he had been, and had visions of getting out of the mist ten years later with ragged clothes and a ten-foot beard.

It sometimes happens that the mist will lie so low on the water that while the driver can see nothing at all someone can stand on the cabin roof and see above the mist, shouting directions down such as, "Look out!" or "Watch where you're going!" or something equally helpful. And someone once told me of standing on the shore and having the weird experience of watching a mast and a red ensign following each other up the lake, with nothing else to be seen, even the deep drone of the engine muffled by the enveloping mist.

CHAPTER 9. War on the Cygnet, and other Campaigns

IN those days I was a keen supporter of "folk music" which was then enjoying something of a revival. Together with some other boatmen who shared a similar appreciation I used to follow one of the local groups, the "Whistling Wallers" as they termed themselves, although unappreciative people said it sounded more like wailing. One of my friends was able to play the guitar, but having nothing more useful in the way of instruments than a drum in my ear, I contented myself with howling quietly in the background.

It was outside one of the Bumblethwaite pubs which catered for this sort of entertainment that my friend and I stumbled upon, or rather over, a crumpled pile of clothing which was lying in the doorway. The pile grunted in pain, and on closer inspection proved to contain a human being, so we dragged it out of the way, propped it up against the wall, and revived it with a pint of ale.

This pile of unkempt humanity was called Barry Evans, and our encounter was the beginning of a lasting friendship. He was short, plump, bespectacled and in his mid-twenties; he had long, unkempt hair and a wild, tangled beard. He described himself as small but beautifully made. By trade Barry was a wandering musician, had no fixed abode and was looking for a job. We were living, he told us, in a gap-toothed society which had made itself too secure to enjoy life and he wanted work which attracted individuals.

"Aha!" my mate promptly informed him. "I know just the job for you." And the next day we introduced him to Captain Wright. Boating - in spite of (or perhaps because of) the poor pay - is something you are supposed to do for love, like farming or working with horses, and attracts all types of individuals from all walks of life; Barry Evans proved to be no exception.

Once he had passed his test and become a fully licensed pilot he did quite well, cruising along with his great mane of hair and beard flying in the breeze in a manner somewhat reminiscent of Meths Maloney, a typical wide grin on his face. Sometimes one could see him perched on his driver's stool using a foot to steer, leaving his hands free to strum a guitar for the benefit of his captive audience.

Barry had been appointed to *Swallow*, a very nondescript sort of launch, and regularly drove it on the morning trip from Boxingdale to Bulswick, arriving very conveniently at opening time, when he would betake himself to the Black Cormorant for half an hour or so, leaving his passengers to fend for themselves. On wet days they would accompany him there as well. One particular morning when it wasn't very busy and we were at something of a loose end we decided to play a prank on him.

As soon as Hevans, as he came to be known, had disappeared up the road and his passengers dispersed about the highways and byways of Bulswick, we took his launch away and tied it up to another pier, round the corner out of sight. When Hevans came back down the road and saw an empty pier he stopped dead in his tracks. We had secreted ourselves in the bushes nearby to watch the fun. We could almost hear his heart thumping against his jacket as he wondered (a) if he had left *Swallow* badly tied up and she had drifted away and (b) if this were so, how was he going to explain it to Captain Wright, and (c) what was he going to do with his passengers meanwhile? As he stood there scratching his head and peering round distractedly, Hevans heard stifled giggles behind a tree. He looked behind it to discover a group of guilty boatmen and chased us all the way along the waterfront, yelling abuse. When he had run out of breath (he wasn't very fit) we took pity on him and told him where to look for his boat. He eventually managed to retrieve it, brought it back to the pier still muttering curses, collected his bemused passengers and set off back for Boxingdale.

This was by no means the last, or the least, of Hevans' misadventures. Before embarking on one of his cruises out of Boxingdale one afternoon he had imbibed an unwise quantity of ale. I say 'unwise' because the first and most basic lesson which every boatman learns is NEVER to drink more than one pint of beer if you are due to sail shortly afterwards, in case you get a sudden call of nature while out on the lake. In those days none of the launches had even heard of toilets, and there aren't any friendly trees out there. Hevans, unfortunately, had not realised this and now saw that, out in the middle of the lake, there was not the remotest possibility of his being able to contain himself until he could get back.

Necessity being the mother of invention, however, he acted with tremendous presence of mind. Pulling alongside the little-used Peartree Pier on the densely wooded Friars Fell shore he tied up, jumped off the boat shouting "Just going to deliver the mail!" to the astonished passengers, and disappeared into the woods waving an envelope over his head.

His misfortunes, however, were by no means over. Having scored nine out of ten for initiative he continued to his next port of call, which was the Fish Park. The Fish Park was a kind of aquarium cum exhibition centre devoted to the fauna and flora of Birblemere; actually it had a very long and official-sounding name, but we called it the Fish Park for short. The pier at this establishment is specially shaped to make it awkward for larger vessels like a passenger launch to land, but we managed it in any case, usually by going across the end.

Hevans, however, missed the pier on his first attempt - or rather hit it and bounced off again, so that he had to back away and try a second time. This time he almost made it but not quite and decided to jump for the pier, rope in hand. At this point he realised his faux pas, for he had left undone those things which he ought to have done. It was reminiscent of Doug MacBride's escapade when landing once at Bulswick in *Crocus* but this was far more serious, for he had landed across the end and left *Swallow* in forward gear, with the bows pointing out towards the lake. Hevans struggled frantically to pull the boat in, at the same time knowing he could never win, and the rope was slipping steadily through his fingers until he reached the back splice at the end. All the while he was shouting at his passengers to switch the damned engine off, but was getting no reaction for naturally they didn't understand his predicament and thought he was having a fit.

At the very last minute, with a terrifying vision of *Swallow* sailing out on her own into the wide blue yonder with passengers aboard, he was spurred to take a desperate leap (rivalling that of MacBride) at *Swallow*'s receding stern and just managed to grab hold of the aft gunwhale while the rest of him hung down over the outside of the boat, up to his waist in water, feet being buffeted dangerously by the propeller wash.

Still the passengers had not moved. They maintained a collective stiff upper lip throughout the entire performance, admiring the scenery while Hevans gibbered with fear, terrified that his legs would get caught in the propeller and emerge in neatly chopped slices in *Swallow*'s wake, till eventually he managed to haul himself slowly and painfully over the stern. When his head appeared over the coaming he found several passengers watching him with interest and one lady enquired, "What's the matter, love?"

Hevans croaked in an anguish both physical and mental, so the lady and her friend succeeded in dragging him aboard, whereat he aborted the mission and returned to Boxingdale. Wet, dripping, bruised, still shaking after his ordeal, he presented such a pitiable sight that his passengers passed a hat round and tipped him handsomely.

This just goes to show to what extraordinary lengths people will go to get a tip.

A week later war was declared on the *Cygnet*. *Cygnet* was an old Mississippi-type paddle steamer (albeit on a smaller scale) which had been purchased by a wealthy river-boat enthusiast and brought with him to Birblemere when he retired. She lay permanently moored in a quiet bay by one of the more distant islands, and we drivers would often sail very close to her during a cruise in order to tell our passengers how she used to carry cowboys, gamblers, negro slaves, loose women and other dubious characters up and down the Mississippi. A lot of them now thought it a pity she didn't carry them up and down Birblemere, to give a bit more local colour, so to speak. Alas, *Cygnet* was now engineless, her paddles had completed their last revolution many years ago, but her paintwork was fully maintained and she made a handsome sight.

The enterprising owner had decided to pay for her upkeep by renting her out to his yuppie friends during the summer, and these rich people would arrive in enormously over-powered speedboats on Friday evenings, sleep aboard over the weekend and spend their time lounging in deck chairs if the weather was fine, reading the Sunday papers and drinking cocktails. It was a matter of local knowledge that their evenings were spent in drunkenness, drug abuse and harlotry.

It happened one Sunday morning that the fellow Locoweed was cruising round the lake with a party of Poles - not fence poles or telegraph poles, but actual Polish people. As was his habit he was telling them all about Birblemere and its surroundings, and a lot more besides. His commentary is famous (perhaps notorious is a better word) and he was not in the slightest way put out by the fact that only three or four of his audience understood English. They could always translate for their friends in any case.

Locoweed halted his boat hard by *Cygnet* and had commenced his harangue when, in full oratorical flow, he was rudely interrupted by a shouted "F--- off!" coming from one of the deckchairs. Once Locoweed had embarked on his commentary, however, he was not easily put off, and though momentarily startled by the unexpected heckling coming from a source not immediately identifiable, carried on louder than ever.

"F--- off! F---- OFF!" came the shout again, this time from more than one voice, and on looking round he noticed that all the yuppies on *Cygnet* were waving their hands at him in gestures whose significance was quite unmistakable. Both gestures and words were understood perfectly well by his passengers, for the language of abuse is universal, and Locoweed had to cut short his commentary and move farther away out of earshot.

On arriving back at Bulswick the passengers complained through their interpreter to Captain Wright about the incident. One gentleman was especially incensed, thinking the whole thing had been aimed at him personally; his name, it turned out, was Mr Focke.

Captain Wright consoled the party and told them such scenes were not a regular occurrence in England, it was only the remnants of the decadent aristocracy trying to cling to their former position. He then in turn complained to the Lake Ranger, and Mr Wall in due course passed this on to the occupants of *Cygnet*. It didn't do much good, however, because from that weekend any of us who stopped in the vicinity of *Cygnet* were subjected to a similar barrage of abuse. Captain Wright thereupon said we weren't to go near the boat in future, but there was no way we drivers were going to take this lying down, and we therefore decided to retaliate.

Every launch from *Mallard* to *Wizard* which found itself in that part of the lake would go deliberately close to *Cygnet*. Boatmen who normally never uttered a word of commentary would stop on every trip and point out the paddle wheels and the funny funnel. Some of the more manoeuvrable launches even went right round the vessel, which had the delightful effect of infuriating the deck-chair brigade to fever pitch, causing them to throw down their newspapers and cocktails and dance a merry jig on the deck. Some of them even chased after us on their speedboats to shout abuse and wave their fists, which we pretended not to notice.

On some mornings a fleet of coaches would arrive from Blackpool for the specific purpose of taking a cruise on Birblemere, and half the fleet was requisitioned to take them. Since we all set out more or less at the same time, we created the effect of a mighty convoy cruising in line ahead, and when we got to where *Cygnet* was moored, what chaos we could create! We would sail right round the vessel, one after the other, each making the turn at the exact spot of the boat in front, each following the leader in true Nelsonian tradition.

Or we would change formation to line abreast, spreading out to advance on an invisible enemy. There were many variations of such formation cruising, the most difficult being two ahead and two astern with one in the middle, forming a group of five. That one impressed the passengers no end. We were therefore all well practised in the forms of naval gambit for attacking *Cygnet*, encouraging the passengers to wave merrily back to the people who were waving at us from the paddle steamer.

When it comes to waving, of course, passengers hardly need any encouragement. It's a funny thing, but when perfectly ordinary, normal, sane people get anywhere near water they turn into compulsive wavers. They wave at everything that moves. We cruise along waving at every boat we pass, at people on the shore, at fishermen, at walkers. They all wave back to us - yachtsmen, water-skiers, picnickers, hikers, you would think we were setting off to cross the Atlantic instead of a one-hour cruise of Birblemere. We wave arms, handkerchiefs, scarves or anything that will serve to attract attention, at perfect strangers, all of whom, caught up in the same strange compulsion, will wave back. Wherever I go on the lake, people wave to me.

It's all rather flattering. Perhaps they think I'm royalty. After years of practice, as a matter of fact, I have developed what is known as the Royal Wave and use it on all occasions but never when passing *Cygnet*. If you want to know how to do the Royal Wave, just watch the Royal Family next time they're on telly; they have a lifetime's experience, and they do it to perfection, with the minimum of exertion and maximum effect.

So there we would set off, half a dozen or so boats, jam-packed with trippers on a Sunday morning cruise, heading in convoy for remote parts of Birblemere to wage war on *Cygnet* - just what we needed to add a little spice to life. We had a particularly daring leader in the person of Hevans, who accomplished three complete circuits of *Cygnet* followed in regular succession by five launches carrying some three hundred passengers amongst them, all waving and cheering and laughing at the deckchair brigade. By the end of the summer the yuppies had hauled down their colours and admitted defeat. There is a limit to how many times a day one can shout "---- off!" without getting bored or out of breath, and we were so obviously enjoying ourselves that they realised it would hurt us more if they just stopped shouting and ignored us.

That season it was my privilege and honour to be given command of *Pegasus*. This was a very fast launch, in fact at that time the fastest in the fleet, and in addition had a manoeuvrability to match her speed. Another advantage was that someone had forgotten to paint her name on the port bow. This meant that if you sailed round *Cygnet* anti-clockwise the deckchair brigade couldn't see a name on the boat in order to complain about her to the Ranger.

Pegasus was not a new boat, in fact she was quite old, you only had to look at the state of the engine case to see that. You see, when passengers board a boat one of them will occasionally slip and bury his teeth in the engine case. Perhaps one in every thousand will do it, and to tell the age of a launch all you have to do is simply to count the number of teethmarks in the woodwork of the engine casing. If there are a great many of them the launch is an old and battle-scarred warrior. If there are very few it is a new boat; or just conceivably has had a new engine case made.

Speaking of people falling on, and off, boats - it never ceases to amaze me how frequently our passengers "have a trip". Getting on they tumble down the steps to pitch face first onto the deck or lock their teeth into the engine casing, while on disembarking you simply wouldn't believe the number of people who place their feet between the pier and the boat and expect an empty space to bear their weight. You've only to watch them clambering slowly and painfully down a couple of steps to realise that in fact the British are a nation of cripples. If you find that hard to believe, look how nimbly a party of foreigners will leap aboard, even the quite elderly ones. They climb all over the seats as well, like a bunch of badly behaved children, but that's a different story.

Pegasus was a spirited and wilful vessel, and was quite capable of starting her own engine on occasion - a clear case of spontaneous combustion. Sometimes I would come down to work in the morning and she would be quietly chugging away at the pier, her fuel tank almost empty. We had to instal a special cut-out switch between the battery and the engine after a patrolling constable had happened along in the early hours of the morning, paused to investigate the running engine and got Captain Wright out of a nice, warm bed just to switch the engine off.

Even worse than spontaneous ignition was her habit of putting herself into gear from time to time. When starting up you had to move the gear lever backwards and forwards until you found the right position for neutral, increase the revs a little, and carry on the incessant battle against spiders or whatever. As the engine warmed up the "neutral" position would alter, and if you failed to adjust the gear lever she would slip into reverse.

One day Bill Birblethwaite had to berth a launch on the outside of *Pegasus*, which was tied next to the pier, started *Pegasus'* engine in order to warm her up, and went off to do something else, not knowing about the boat's little idiosyncrasy.

He returned just in time to hear a loud 'crack!' as *Pegasus'* rope parted, to stand and watch in open-mouthed amazement as she began reversing out into the bay with the other launch still tied alongside. Everyone started shouting and rushing about in different directions, as people do when there is a panic on, some dashing for the nearest launch to set off in pursuit of the runaways. Captain Wright dived into a nearby rowing boat, presumably to commit suicide, for the launches would have gored him had he managed to get close enough, while poor Bill just stood and gaped. Pursuit however turned out to be unnecessary, for *Pegasus* did not reverse out in a straight line but started to swing round in a circle as her rudder jammed hard over and was now heading across to the far side of the bay where somebody's private pier stuck out into the lake. Both boats reached this pier before help could arrive, and now travelled along it bouncing from post to post, and would run aground any minute.

It was Hevans who saved the situation. He'd just emerged from the public toilets which were situated not far from this little pier, still half asleep and rubbing his eyes, obviously trying to recover from the evening before. Everyone screamed frantically at him because he was the only person in a position to do something about the situation.

Amazingly, he woke to the realisation of what was going on, ran over to the small pier, leapt down onto *Pegasus* and disengaged the gear lever; then he switched the engine off. He was only just in time, too, because as Pegasus and its neighbour slowed to a halt they both touched bottom simultaneously, having by now run out of lake.

Young Hevans was the hero of the day - well, of the hour. Captain Wright was so pleased that when the boats had been rescued and brought back to port he went up to Hevans, shook his hand, and tipped him a shilling. A whole shilling! That, of course, was in the days before decimalisation.

In spite of this *Pegasus* was never Hevans' favourite boat. This was on account of her once having played a dirty trick on him. He'd got a full load of passengers, received the 'Go Away' signal, and set off astern but travelling much too fast. It was a cold morning, and he was wearing his old ankle-length greatcoat.

As the propeller suddenly gripped the water the pressure on the rudder increased violently and whipped the wheel from his grasp. It flew over to full lock and the spokes caught in his greatcoat as it went, taking him with it. With a cry of mingled surprise and terror Hevans was jerked right off his feet and ended up with his head in one passenger's lap and his feet protruding horizontally beyond the opposite side of the engine case. A highly amusing predicament, at least for anyone who was watching, except that Hevans now couldn't reach the throttle from where was hanging and thus faced the prospect of reversing *Pegasus* right round the bay and up the beach - and so having to give Captain Wright his shilling back. He had to reach the throttle in order to slow down, and he had to slow down in order to disentangle himself from the wheel.

Once again, Hevans acted in the nick of time, literally tearing himself out of his greatcoat, buttons flying everywhere, hauled himself to his feet and closed the throttle just in time. The passengers applauded loudly, one gentleman saying he hadn't laughed as much since V.E. day. Hevans, however, didn't see the joke.

He did, on another occasion, have a laugh at Captain Wright's expense. He had been put on *Gannet*, her regular skipper being absent that day from a bout of 'tertian ague', which is another way of describing a hangover. Captain Wright had loaded the boat with passengers and then sent Hevans out on a cruise. Hevans had no sooner rounded Shuttleworth Nab than *Gannet's* engine coughed once or twice, then died away completely. There was an embarrassing silence, broken only by the sound of waves gently lapping against the hull as *Gannet* glided gracefully onwards at a gently decreasing rate of knots. In fact she had just enough way on her (it was a calm day) for Hevans to steer to a halt at the nearest pier, where he thankfully tied up.

Finding himself a mere five minutes' walk away from Bulswick, he instructed his passengers to remain on board and not to stray along the shore and get lost, while he went in search of a rescue launch. And so, five minutes later, there was Captain Wright busy loading a boat for the next cruise when whom should his jaundiced eye light upon but Hevans himself strolling nonchalantly along the waterfront.

He half turned away, froze momentarily, then whipped round and shrieked in a tone of rising hysteria: "Wh.... what are you doing here, Hevans? I sent you out ten minutes ago! Where's *Gannet*?"

Hevans waited until the distraught fellow had calmed down a bit, and explained the situation, thoroughly enjoying himself in the meantime. The problem was solved by dispatching two more boats in the wake of *Gannet* (lucky there were two to spare!) - one to take the passengers on the rest of their cruise, assuming they still wanted to go, the other to tow *Gannet* back into port.

Most of them voted to carry on with the cruise, although you'd have thought they'd by now have had enough of sitting at the pier for half an hour or so waiting to be rescued, helpless under the inquisitive gaze of passing strollers or curious speedboats. The few who wanted to abort the cruise also wanted their money back, something Captain Wright was extremely reluctant to give them.

Hevans went down in history as being the only boatman ever to have (a) deserted his command while having passengers aboard, and (b) returned from a cruise on foot.

CHAPTER 10. Birth of a *Rose*

ONE morning Captain Wright called me into his office. You normally don't get called into the office unless you've done something wrong, but my conscience was clear at that time. I hadn't sunk any yachts recently, hadn't swamped any cabin cruisers, hadn't even driven over a water-skier. So wondering what it could all be about, I stepped within the hallowed portals.

Captain Wright was brandishing a picture postcard. "What do you think of this, Brian?"

When he'd finished waving it about I took it from him and had a look. Very attractive scene - a lake in the Alps, all blue water with snow-clad peaks as a backdrop. In the foreground was a rather modern-looking cruiser - I forget the name of the boat, I forget even the name of the lake - Garda or Maggiore, perhaps.

"Very nice," I replied. "Who do we know who's on holiday out there?"

"Well, it's my wife's cousin - but anyway, they sent me this postcard. Rather attractive, don't you think?"

"Not bad-looking," I agreed, wondering what was coming next.

"Not the girl on the bow, the *boat*. Now, how do you think one of these would look on Birblemere?"

"You can't be serious," I told him.

"No, probably cost a fortune. Still, people would pay good money to get on one of these."

I left him still staring at the postcard. A boat like that in the Lakes! Whatever next? Might as well plan a manned space shot to Mars!

I thought no more about it until a couple of weeks later, when David Duckworth happened to mention that his father, semi-retired Chairman Fred, had just had a long talk with Captain Wright.

"I think they're serious about getting another boat," he told me.

"What, another *Merganser*? Or a new *Pandora*?"

"No, no, nothing like that. Something continental, like that thing on the postcard."

I stared. "Never."

"Oh yes. I know for a fact someone's flying out to Holland next month to have a look. There's a firm over there that builds these kind of boats."

"It would cost a fortune."

"There's such things as bank loans, you know."

Flying to Holland? Business on the Continent? My goodness, Bulswick & Lake Launch Services was going big-time now - what had happened to the quiet, family firm I had once known, which until only a few years ago had been run by a handful of retired boat-builders and fishermen?

The answer came just twelve months later, about halfway down the M6 in David's car. A few of us had gone out to meet the firm's brand-new supercruiser as she made her slow and sedate way up the motorway. Not, I hasten to add, under her own power but towed along on a low-loader. We parked on a convenient bridge overlooking the busy route where we could have a good view of the new arrival, and settled down to wait. To pass the time David had brought a thermos and sandwiches, and it was a pleasant spring evening.

Of course, these things always take time - nothing anticipated in hope ever arrives when it's expected. People kept glancing at watches, asking: "Where is it? What's happened?" Had we got the right day? Had we got the right route? But eventually our new boat hove into sight. Heralded by a police car with flashing light, there she came at a nice, sedate fifteen miles an hour, huge and white and gleaming. We were all breathless with awe.

David just stared as she sailed by beneath us, for all the world as if she were actually floating on water.

"Good Lord!" he exclaimed. "How on earth am I going to drive a thing that size? She'll never get round Ross Holmé."

And for all his professional ability, I think he was genuinely worried. The boat was huge. She was designed to carry over two hundred passengers who were accommodated on two decks. She had power steering and twin screws, and none of us had ever driven a boat with two engines before. She even had a bar - and that was another, by no means unwelcome, novelty. She was as far advanced above the old *Wizard*, for example, as an Intercity 125 was above Stephenson's Rocket.

David needn't have worried. *Lakeland Rose,* as Captain Wright christened her, was a dream to drive: pure joy itself.

There was an old slipway near Bulswick at which our new cruiser presently arrived, and was parked overnight for launching the next day. A cluster of boatmen gathered round her, awed at the sight, for out of the water her massive bulk quite dwarfed her surroundings. There was no way aboard except by ladder, but once inside the main saloon we were overwhelmed by the smell of newness - the plush seating, the impression of space and light, the huge steering wheel and gleaming controls. The control panel was so full of knobs and instruments and gauges you would need a handbook to find your way round. (As a matter of fact, a handbook *did* turn up, but it was all in Dutch and therefore not much use to anyone).

But what impressed everyone more than anything else were the huge, gleaming, engine telegraphs - just like on the bridge of a proper ship. David gripped the polished brass handles and a strange, faraway look came into his eyes.

The next morning Mrs Wright duly cracked a bottle of champagne across her bows and *Lakeland Rose* slid smoothly down the slipway and into the tranquil waters of Birblemere Both engines started beautifully first time (an engineer had obligingly come over from Holland just to make sure everything went smoothly) and it was with Captain Wright himself at the helm that the boat glided quietly out into the bay on that sunlit spring morning..... harbinger of a new era.

We went off on a tour of the lake - Captain and Mrs Wright, myself, David Duckworth, half the other drivers who weren't actually ferrying passengers around, one or two crewboys and a few assorted individuals who were associated with the firm in varying degrees. David stood beside his boss, itching to be at the wheel and feel the tremor of the engines beneath his own fingers, but Captain Wright wasn't having any of it - this was his boat, he'd paid for her, and he was going to get his money's worth.

Kees, the Dutch engineer, opened the engine room door and showed me the engines, huge marine diesels painted a bright, metallic blue. The noise when the soundproof door was opened was truly deafening, Captain Wright shouted to me to shut it, he couldn't hear himself think. What a blessed silence prevailed when I closed it again, the ear-shattering roar turning instantly into a subdued murmur.

We went on an extended cruise nearly all the way round Birblemere, calling at Boxingdale on the way, where the older boatmen stared with disbelief at this gleaming white monster which had suddenly descended in their midst.

The maiden voyage of *Lakeland Rose* (ie. with fare-paying

passengers) took place the very next day - the management couldn't wait to bring her into service. David was at the helm, feeling just a little bit nervous because he had a V.I.P. aboard in the person of Sir Archibald Globus. Sir Archibald (knighted for services to tourism) was the director of the Birblemere Navigation Board, a tall, silver-haired gentleman who 'ran' Birblemere as if it were his own private fiefdom - which, for all practical purposes, it was. He controlled everything - launch cruise fares, private moorings, every activity from angling to yachting, from duck-shooting to parascending - the lot.

Captain Wright, in the presence of Sir Archibald, was obsequiousness itself, because even he knew what side his bread was buttered on - if he were ever to put a foot wrong, B.&L.L.S. could be shut down the very next day on the mere say-so of Sir Archibald.

So the director of the Birblemere Navigation Board sat just behind David, where he had a good view of the steering wheel, and watched impassively as David put the boat through its evolutions. Fortunately, she handled perfectly. Her twin screws and power steering gave her the necessary manoeuvrability to land and reverse out from the narrow confines of the bay, she could turn in less than her own length, and even the wind was no problem.

Let me explain. You may by now have thought it easy enough to handle a boat..... just put the engine astern, glide away from the pier until you've got sufficient room to perform a turn, then go ahead, put the wheel over the opposite way, and bingo! You're on your way. And when you come back in to land, just slow down, go astern as you come alongside, and Bob's your uncle. That's how things are supposed to work under ideal circumstances, but we all know things never run as they should.

What, for instance, happens when there's a gale blowing you away from the pier as you come alongside? You've got to position your boat at the correct angle, but with the wind pushing you away - sometimes quite forcefully - that angle keeps changing all the time as you make your approach. The answer is often to come in faster than normal and reverse hard - keeping your fingers crossed that the engine will stop the boat in time, won't cut out or do something equally silly. (Remember *Suzanne's* propeller dropping off?) This may sound incredible nowadays, but when I first started driving there were boats - like the *Wizard* - which would do just that.

Fortunately the more modern launches have diesel engines which are far more reliable, which is just as well because if *Lakeland Rose* tried to land against the wind and her engine cut out at the crucial moment nothing - but nothing - could stop her from simply demolishing the harbour wall. She weighed forty tons and had a top speed of twelve and a half knots, and you don't stop a boat that size just by winding a rope round a post.

Anyway, it was a smooth, calm day for Sir Archibald's cruise, nothing went wrong, and on disembarking that dignitary congratulated David on his superb handling of the boat and went away well pleased with the firm's new attraction. And what's more, because the engine was still being run in, David only drove *Lakeland Rose* very cautiously and she made hardly any wash, which seemed to please Sir Archibald no end. Still, it was very nice of him, especially as he hadn't paid a penny for his ticket.

Lakeland Rose quickly became a familiar sight on Birblemere as she cruised up and down the lake, visiting places like Biskey Landing or Boxingdale, sailing round Ross Holme, calling at the Oaktree Hotel or the Fish Park, and other sundry points. Lots of people thought she was built of fibreglass and asked what we were going to do with her in the winter, in case Birblemere froze over. A fibreglass hull would be crushed in the ice.

But the *Rose* was solid steel, as you'd soon find out if you dropped anything in the bilges, when a mighty clang would reverberate through the entire ship. Ice? She'd grind her way through anything a Birblemere winter could offer, as if she'd been tailor-made for the job.

Our new boat was enormously popular - so popular in fact that she began to make the other launches - *Pegasus, Gannet, Mallard*, etc. - seem redundant; even *Merganser* was now a bit old-fashioned, and look what a novelty she'd been in her day! David found he was now spending all his time on the lake, for no sooner had the *Rose* landed from one cruise and her passengers been disgorged than Captain Wright was loading her up again for the next cruise, sometimes the pier was even groaning under the weight of people queueing. When David complained about having to go out all the time, Captain Wright sarcastically enquired if he'd prefer to go back to *Mallard*, there were plenty of volunteers to skipper this prestigious new vessel. Of course, David would never dream of allowing himself to be displaced in this way.

Lakeland Rose sailed sometimes with up to half a dozen crew members aboard - the skipper, a mate who could steer from time to time and looked after the ropes when she berthed, a crewboy to look after the stern rope and help in the bar, a barmaid (Captain Wright's teenage daughter, Penny) and, for the first couple of weeks, the Dutch engineer Kees who would keep an eye on all the machinery. And believe me, those engines needed an awful lot of attention, especially while they were running in. But once run in, they ran sweet and true and never gave a moment's bother.

One afternoon when it was quiet (ie. raining) Kees said he'd like to take the governors off both engines and let them have their heads. So he did, and David opened both throttles to full ahead, just to see what *Lakeland Rose* could do.

We stood there amazed. The gentle hum from the engine room altered to a deep-throated roar; the boat's bows rose up into the air as the pressure beneath the hull altered, and away she went, transformed from a peaceful pleasure cruiser to something resembling a destroyer laying depth charges. There was a great hissing of spray from beneath the bows, and two standing waves could be seen on either beam. I went aft to see what the view was like from the stern: all you could see was a mountain of creamy water fountaining up from beneath the transom, while the deck plates beneath my feet trembled with the power, and the propeller shafts whined and groaned with the stress.

Returning forrard, I had to claw my way up from seat to seat, thinking that if they were going to run the boat at this speed, they'd better provide mountaineering equipment for the passengers, since the deck was inclined at such a steep angle.

Kees signalled to David to ease the throttles back. "Not good. Not good," he said, wagging his finger. "Too fast. You drive like this too long, and engine blow up. Not good."

And shaking his head, he disappeared back into the engine room to readjust the governors. But we could tell he was pleased, all the same, with they way those beautiful engines had performed. Later that day, however, we got a complaint that a fishing boat on the other side of Birblemere had been swamped with the wash from *Lakeland Rose*. Captain Wright of course denied all knowledge.

It was nice knowing all that power was lying there in reserve, even if we never needed to travel that fast on Birblemere ever again. It certainly put boats like *Pegasus* and *Pride of Raasay* in the shade. That set me thinking of Boxer Bill. I wonder if he ever did end up in Patagonia, as rumoured? When I thought back to all those years when he had terrorised our little fleet with his open ambushes on *Pride* - what a revenge we could have had now with our *Rose*! I'd have loved to see the expression on Boxer's face as our fast new cruiser left him rolling in our wake!

One of the comments we heard quite frequently went something like this: "Oh, this is just like one of those boats they have in Amsterdam. Perhaps they take you round the harbour and give you a commentary in all those languages!"

No madam, we do not take you round the harbour, we take you on a scenic cruise of Birblemere whence you may watch the landscape floating serenely by, past Shuttleworth Nab, round Ross Holme and the other islands following the wooded shoreline of Friars Fell, with glances at Oaktree Hotel and the Fish Park and perhaps a call at Boxingdale. You'll get your commentary, but it will be in English, and what's more English spoken with a strong northern accent, none of your lar-di-da 'received' southern pronunciation - and none of your gabbling in half a dozen different languages which would drive everyone else mad in two minutes flat. Our northern accent (and I had learned to speak like a northerner despite having been born in the south-east) was at times so strong that foreigners (eg. Scots or Americans) would sometimes complain they couldn't understand us.

Lakeland Rose proved so successful that a couple of years later Captain Wright felt sufficiently confident to order a couple more cruisers from Holland. These, however, were much smaller boats (although still dwarfing launches like *Merganser*) with only a single deck and a single screw. They did however attract the crowds as much as the *Rose* - perhaps it was because so many people had seen these boats on the Dutch canals that they were amazed to behold them on Birblemere. Others, having asked where the *Rose* and her sister ships had been built, were overcome with patriotic indignation and asked why such beautiful cruisers couldn't be built in Britain. Captain Wright might have told them they *could* be built in Britain, it's just that the price, and the delivery time, made no economic sense.

Other passengers asked how the boats were brought to Birblemere. David used to tell them they were first assembled in Holland, tested on the canals, then taken to bits again with each part carefully numbered, shipped over as a 'build-it-yourself' kit and reassembled on the shores of Birblemere. Some of them believed even that.

Yet others asked how on earth they managed to get her mast underneath the motorway bridges. David solved that one by persuading them the height of each bridge was carefully measured, and then a couple of feet of stonework was removed so that *Lakeland Rose* might pass beneath, to be cemented back into place after she'd passed by. From the number of people who believed, or appeared to believe, that one, David was able to prove part of Abraham Lincoln's famous dictum, that you can fool some of the people all of the time.

CHAPTER 11. Microphones, and their Abuses

SOME years ago a driver with a rather inventive turn of mind had fitted *Pegasus* out with a microphone and loudspeakers. This was to enable him to talk to his passengers without having to leave the wheel and point out everything twice over - once to those in the front, and once to those in the cabin. The entire apparatus was a Heath Robinson contraption, with two speakers in the cabin and one in the bows. This latter was detachable so that it could be removed for the night, or in case of rough weather, and concealed in the bow locker. Yards of cable wound its way underneath the floorboards and connected with a small microphone on the control panel. The thing had never worked properly: the passengers in the cabin could only hear a whisper through the speakers, while people sitting in the first four seats of the bow were practically deafened by the solitary speaker there. The rest of the passengers were considerably closer to the engine than to the speakers, and consequently heard more of the engine and less of the commentary.

During the time when *Pegasus* was under my command I hardly ever used the microphone for the purpose for which it was intended. It was far easier to halt the boat in open water and talk to them twice, at least that way they could all hear what I was saying, and were therefore more likely to cough up with the gratuities. This is not to say, however, that the microphone was no use at all. Far from it; I evolved a little game to play using the microphone whenever I felt bored and there was a suitable subject - usually a child - sitting next to the cable locker.

This was where the loudspeaker was concealed, and there was nothing at all to indicate its presence. Usually I never had long to wait because children always dive straight for the very front of the boat when they get on. During the cruise I would switch the loudspeaker control over to the front one only, so that nothing could be heared in the cabin, then taking care I was unobserved, I would secrete the microphone up my sleeve and whisper into it: "Help! Help! Let me out!"

If you pitched the volume just right the child sitting next to the cable locker would be the only one to hear this curious call. He usually looked at the locker, then at the other passengers, and getting no reaction from them would look at me. I would meanwhile be gazing at the distant horizon in complete unconcern.

When the little boy had settled down I would do it again and he would turn and glare at me suspiciously. The funniest reaction, hilarious through the sheer injustice of it, was when after hearing repeated cries for help from the cable locker, the lad would turn to his parents. "Dad, dad, there's someone trapped in there! Listen!" Dad listens and nothing at all happens, while I am to be found gazing innocently at the scenery whenever he looks at me. Dad says: "Rubbish! There's no-one there," and dismisses the subject from his mind.

Two minutes later that whispered cry comes again: "Help! Let me out!"

"Dad, there IS someone there! I heard them!"

Nothing again when Dad listens. "Shut up and don't be silly," says Dad.

"Help! Please help me!"

"Dad! Listen!"

And then Dad gets very cross and gives the poor lad a clip over the ear and I fall off my stool laughing.

Sometimes a child would actually open the bow locker out of uncontrollable curiosity - but adults do this as well - only to be confronted with the circular end of a large fuel tank, on which was depicted the following illustration:

This had been painted by some wit who had worked on the boat in ages past, presumably to enjoy the momentary discomfort of curious persons who couldn't resist opening the locker door to see what lay within.

Nowadays, of course, we are all used to the various public address systems which have been installed in the newer boats - used to them, that is, but not necessarily practised in their use. Contrary to popular belief, there is more to using a public address than simply talking to people in a conversational tone, which merely comes over as a confused jumble of words with very little meaning.

The most common fault in using a microphone is to shout down it; the noise coming out of the other end is absolutely horrible. Neither must you hold the mike too close to your mouth, for this will distort your words, nor must it be too far away from your mouth, or your audience will not hear you. You have to speak quite slowly and very clearly, in short bursts of no more than a few seconds in order to obtain the best results.

Everyone has their own individual style of delivery. Some people will never learn how to use the thing properly: for instance one driver would briefly point with outstretched arm (the arm holding the microphone) at the object of interest he was describing. This was effective in directing the gaze of the passengers the right way, but the information was curiously fragmented. "Over there to your right, ladies and... ancient paddle... and loose women... in use now." But I suppose that is better than the fellow who talked into the microphone for the whole wretched cruise, a continuous and monotonous monologue interrupted only by his need to pause for breath. Nobody knew what he found to talk about.

There was a crewman one season who used to walk up and down the gangway relating local ghost stories to his passengers - especially in the evenings or during stormy weather when we were cruising along the Friars Fell shore. He'd tell them the tale about the ghost of the friar seen flitting silently through the trees, and hold them all spellbound. Never had I enjoyed a cruise so peaceful, what with the drone of the engine and the drone from the practised storyteller: I often longed to burst a paper bag with a bang and watch them all jump overboard with fright.

Some drivers try to make their passengers smile by giving humorous commentaries. This is a dangerous practice because today's audiences are all so sophisticated, and used to seeing professional entertainers on television. If one's jokes fall flat as they can so easily do, the skipper ends up feeling exceedingly foolish.

For example, you could start off by testing their geography: "Good morning, ladies and gentlemen. Welcome to Loch Lomond, the island on your right is completely surrounded by water."

Then you look round to judge the reaction. If they are all looking stone-faced at the said island you can kick the commentary into touch and forget the jokes. If, however, they laugh you have a created a pleasant atmosphere for the rest of the cruise. The joke may be feeble, but the laughter means you have got their attention, and can go ahead with the commentary. One skipper, when crossing the widest part of Birblemere, always announced sternly: "We are now crossing over the deepest point of the lake, ladies and gentlemen, the water here reaches a depth of over five hundred feet. Now I hope you're all enjoying the cruise. No complaints, I trust?" I never risked that one in case there were.

For young drivers who are new to the job and nervous about speaking in public, giving a commentary can be something of an ordeal. We once had a very shy young man, a university student named Charles Temple-Meads. During his first season on the lake he was far too embarrassed to say anything at all. By his second season, however, he had been encouraged to talk a little, and was sent off one day to collect a party of New Zealanders from that well-known pick-up point, the Oaktree Hotel. New Zealanders are friendly people and easy to get on with, and Captain Wright particularly wanted to create a good impression with this cruise in the hope that it would become a regular booking. He therefore went to the trouble of actually *writing* out a commentary for Charles, and sent him on his way with kindly words of encouragement.

Charles started off very seriously, at first reading carefully from his prepared script, but his passengers were friendly and appreciative so that after a while he began to forget his nervousness and departed from his set commentary. He waxed lyrical; he began to tell them a variety of doubtful stories he had heard from other boatmen, all of which went down very well indeed.

When they arrived back at the Oaktree Hotel the pier was full of holiday-makers on their cruisers, water-skiers relaxing between sorties, people sunbathing whilst enjoying drinks sent down from the hotel. Charles was very careful with his landing in order not to make a fool of himself in front of all these people, which was not easy due to the somewhat constricted mooring space on the pier. Anyway, he landed and tied up in the correct manner, hoping that as his commentary had gone down so well his passengers would not stint on the gratuities. A self-appointed spokesman for the party then stood up and delivered a short speech (which was overheard by all and sundry) about the excellence of the trip and the brilliance of the commentary, all due to the wonderful skipper who had done so much to make it as enjoyable as he could for them; and would they please show their appreciation in the usual manner. Charles blushed furiously as every eye turned in his direction; but there was more to come.

To his surprise and horror the entire party, far from digging deep into their pockets, stood up and gave him a long round of applause (applause, prolonged applause, ovation, standing ovation, all stand) and then burst into "For He's a Jolly Good Fellow" for an agonising five minutes. And it was such a rousing ovation he got that not only were the New Zealanders applauding, but the amused spectators on the cruisers and the resting water-skiers on their speedboats joined in as well, grinning their heads off and entering into the general spirit of the thing, while Charles wished he could make himself invisible. He even contemplated lifting up a floorboard and hiding in the bilges, but they would have dragged him out again.

He never gave a commentary again, ever.

I once had a crewman for a couple of seasons by the name of Barry Bateman; he was a retired grave-digger. Barry scorned the use of a microphone for commentaries, and as a consequence was one of the best crews I ever had as far as passenger relations were concerned. He was a born entertainer with a natural warmth and outgoing personality which made him an instant hit even with the dourest of parties, and you wondered why he'd ever taken up grave-digging in the first place. You have only got your passengers for an hour or so, first impressions are the only impressions you have time for, and Barry excelled at first impressions. He would walk up and down the boat smiling at all and sundry (and meaning it), a word or two here, a joke there, and sooner or later he would burst into song. The surprised passengers, after a few minutes to get over the shock, would join in, and off we would go singing "Cruising Down the River", "My Bonnie Lies Over the Ocean", "Daisy, Daisy" and other favourites, led by Barry's rich tenor. The concert could heard right along the shore as we cruised by, and in a good part of Bulswick as well, if the wind was in the right direction.

This all went to show that a singing ship is a happy ship, and I never knew a man so consistently good-natured as Barry. A skipper and his crew are constantly in each other's company, perhaps get on each other's nerves from time to time, but I am indebted to Mr

Bateman for his unfailing good humour, he kept me as cheerful as he did the passengers.

Public address systems, however, can have their disadvantages. If, for instance, your crew is giving the commentary you have to listen to it, word for word, day in and day out, right through the season, which can become rather tedious since you have taught him what to say in the first place and have heard it all before - many, many times, mistakes included. So you close your mind to it, at the same time half listening in the hope that he will mess it all up and so relieve the monotony.

David Duckworth once had a truly awful experience on *Lakeland Rose*. During the school holidays we occasionally get schoolboys coming down to earn a few pennies by serving as extra crew - casting off ropes, catching us in as we land, etc. It so happened that a young teenager, Martin Merryweather (a great grand-nephew of old George Merryweather of Biskey Landing), was crewing with David one weekend. This wretched youth was just going through a phase of being fascinated by the idea of homosexuality, and quite suddenly when he and David were out on the lake, without any warning whatsoever, he picked up the microphone and before the astonished skipper could do anything, announced to the passengers: "Ladies and gentlemen, the driver's gay."

How do you handle a thing like that? Ignore it - and by your silence imply acceptance of the statement? Deny it over the public address? - "Ladies and gentlemen, this is the driver speaking. I am NOT gay."

Impossible.

David made one of those rapid decisions which we all have to make from time to time, and it cured the precocious youth of attempting further pranks for a very long time afterwards. Leaping from his driver's seat he caught Merryweather a terrific clout over the head, then seized the half-stunned youth, opened the engine-room door, bundled him inside, and locked it behind him. *Lakeland Rose*'s engine-room is dark, hot and incredibly noisy with the roar of two large and powerful diesels revving at close on full speed. It was here that the young Merryweather was forced to spend the remainder of that cruise and was let out when they'd landed looking suitably chastened. Pale, trembling and partially deafened, he was informed by his still incensed captain that if he ever tried on anything like that again, it would be curtains for him. David meant it, and Merryweather believed him.

One of the passengers who had witnessed all this turned to

David on leaving the boat and said, "Well done, lad! You handled that just right. If it'd been me, I'd have thrown the beggar overboard!"

Some of the launches (the more recent ones) have a device whereby a cassette player can be coupled up to the public address. In this way it is possible to pre-record a commentary, and once you have got the hang of it, there is no denying it forms a very useful aid. David was the first to start experimenting with taped commentaries - he never liked having to give them in any case. The important thing to remember with these is that you must go round Birblemere in the same way as the points of interest come up on the tape. Having got that right, the driver must then know how many such places are mentioned, and when to switch the tape on and when to switch it off. If you start day-dreaming and forget to switch on an item, you have had it for the rest of the cruise, for the commentary will be one viewpoint behind. Perhaps for many passengers this would not make all that much difference, although you might feel rather foolish if you started telling them about Rosthwaite Keep while circumnavigating the *Cygnet*.

David was so enthusiastic about cassette tapes that he used to keep quite a collection in his locker, and would often play a selection to his passengers while the boat was waiting to sail. Perhaps David's taste in music didn't always coincide with that of the general public, because one day someone complained to Captain Wright about having to listen to "Twilight of the Gods" whilst cruising round the islands.

When taking *Lakeland Rose* you had to be very careful to play only the tape labelled "Cruise Commentary". By inadvertently taking the wrong one, I have treated my passengers to everything from Beeethoven Quartets to Teach Yourself Chinese (that was the year David took his wife on an Oriental tour). The most popular tape was Scott Joplin, I was often requested to leave it on, the passengers preferring ragtime to cruise commentaries. But then even this novelty wore off after a while, and I returned to live commentaries through the mike. None of your tinned stuff for *my* passengers, they get theirs fresh.

Our most accomplished microphone performer was undoubtedly the fellow Locoweed. He might not have been up to much as a launch driver, but by golly! his commentaries took some beating. Nobody ever gave a commentary quite like Locoweed's, and he would vary his format so often that it never grew stale. He talked throughout the entire cruise, which was all very well, but occasionally he would start to think about what he was actually saying and come out with some awful blunders. On one occasion he was relating how the water board extracted water from Birblemere to supply the industrial conurbations farther south "...for drinking purposes," as he put it, ending with the immortal line, "...to thirst Manchester's never-ending quench." And he never even noticed his blunder.

Locoweed's competence as a crewman was in inverse ratio to his ability as a commentator. He had a certain air about him that suggested: "Don't worry, you are in safe hands, I have everything under control." The trouble was that he hadn't. He would walk purposefully down the pier to catch a boat in and would then get it all wrong. The rope would come off the cleat, or he would tie it to the wrong post, or throw it in the lake, or something. We used to cringe when we saw him coming to help us.

Somehow he used to get into a frightful tangle when commentating, like a kind of Houdini in reverse. One evening during a short break in the proceedings he removed a pipe from the top pocket of his jacket, put the microphone away temporarily in the same pocket, and started filling his pipe with tobacco. At this point a passenger sitting four seats back asked a question, so Locoweed set his pipe down on the dashboard - thinking it was a microphone - and set off down the gangway to answer the query. When the coiled telephone-type cable attached to the mike had stretched to its limit the instrument shot out of his pocket and crashed to the deck with a tremendous bang which reverberated round and round the entire boat, because he had left it switched on. Having retrieved it from the deck and answered the question, he sat down again on his perch near the wheel and replaced it in his top pocket.

Five minutes later as we approached the next point of interest, Locoweed reached for his pipe which lay on the dashboard and started talking into it. Realising his error and now thrown completely off his stride, he put the pipe down again, fumbled for his lighter, took the microphone from his top pocket and tried to set fire to it as he brought it towards his mouth. At that point I gently removed it from his grasp, told him to go away and have a smoke, and resumed the commentary myself.

All this goes to show that public address systems can be very useful if handled properly, but to the untrained operator they are fraught with hazards.

CHAPTER 12. Ship to Shore

ALL that business with microphones, cassettes and commentaries pales into insignificance compared with the fun we had when the firm decided to introduce ship-to-shore communications. To see how this came about we have to go back some time to a peaceful summer's afternoon on Birblemere when you're coming in after a gentle cruise round the lake, thinking "just one more trip then it'll be time to go home". So you come round the corner past those old, familiar, green-painted boathouses to be greeted by a scene of sheer, absolute chaos.

Lakeland Rose is backing away from one jetty, *Mallard* from another. As well as yourself, two or three other boats are trying to land at the same time, and from different directions, so you could have as many as half a dozen large launches manoeuvring simultaneously in a confined space, some going ahead, some astern, some trying to berth, some trying to leave.

Meanwhile Captain Wright is at the end of the pier doing a merry dance as he tries to indicate which boat has to land where, wielding a boathook as if it were a conductor's baton, and our little fleet an entire symphony orchestra which he is taking through a full-dress rehearsal. He jumps in the air, he shouts, he waves his arms, he gestures with his boathook; and nobody takes a blind bit of notice because we're all too busy watching what the other boats are doing - will the skipper turn to port or starboard? - because in that confined channel with so many craft to-ing and fro-ing the Birblemere Navigation Rules have for all practical purposes ceased to apply.

Two launches get tangled together. Locoweed charges backwards and forwards in a panic of indecision and manages to bend a pier post. Eventually everyone gets sorted out, Captain Wright goes back to selling tickets to prospective passengers, peace is restored for a while to the ruffled waters of the bay. There is nothing new about this kind of performance, we've undergone it many times before, and we hardened seadogs are quite used to it.

It was round about this time that CB was legalised and one winter (this being a slack time of the year) the firm purchased a couple of sets just by way of experiment. No, this wasn't the real, genuine, marine band affair, it was something out of the local toyshop, as you might expect. One was set up in *Crocus*, the other in our office on the beach. When all was ready and we'd decided what channel we were going to use, Captain Wright told me to stand by the set in the boat while he went over to the office to call me. His message came through loud and clear: "Hello Crocus. Hello Crocus. This is Captain Wright. Are you receiving me? Over."

All in best radio style as popularised by innumerable TV series. Entering into the spirit of the thing, I immediately took up the handset and replied, "Hello Captain Wright, this is *Crocus*. I am on fire and sinking. Repeat, I am on fire and sinking. Require immediate assistance. Over."

There came a kind of strangled choking noise over the airwaves and then silence. Seconds later a distraught manager flew out of the office and across the beach. "Brian, for Heaven's sake, NEVER say anything like that over the air. You don't know who might be listening. Anybody could have picked that up, anybody at all. Why, they might even be on to the police this very moment!"

"Calm down," I told him. "Everything's in order." And to make certain, I appended the following broadcast: "Hello all stations, hello all stations. This is *Crocus*. I am NOT on fire and am NOT sinking. Repeat, I am NOT on fire and am NOT sinking. Over."

There was dead silence from the receiver. Not even a crackle. I often wondered what use the thing might be in a genuine emergency.

In time we all got used to the thing; we grew to know and love our friendly CB. Radio discipline was unheard of. Of course, you'd always get the type who'd spent N years in the navy and thought he knew how to run the firm, but we always put people like him very firmly in their place. We ended up having lots of fun with irrelevant conversations echoing round and round the fleet. The CB was a great gossip manufacturer and we'd relay messages to each other if boats were operating in radio black spots - and believe me, Birblemere was full of such black spots. "David, your wife's going out and you'll have to make your own tea."

"Oh good, I think I'll nip up to the Cormorant for a pint or two and then try the Chinese takeaway. Anyone fancy a drink when we finish?"

"Sorry, I'm on late shift tonight."

"*Mallard* here. Yes, see you up there, David."

And from the base station: "Will you just be quiet, you lot, we're trying to run a business back here." That would be Captain Wright trying to answer the phone and sell tickets at the same time.

But of course there was another side to it all. Since it was CB, we were on open channel all the time, and from time to time strangers would butt in on our conversations. Normally we'd tell them, more or less politely, to go away - but that's a double-edged weapon, they knew who we were and what we were doing and could play havoc with our radio traffic if they really wanted to. But usually they were too far away to receive our rather weak transmissions, although we could hear their much more powerful broadcasts loud and clear. I remember one Bank Holiday we got someone broadcasting from abroad:

"Germany calling. Germany calling...." For a horrifying moment I thought we were getting a delayed echo from the Second World War. "Hello England, this is Germany calling. My name is Hans and I am transmitting from Hamburg on...." and there would follow a load of technical information which nobody understood. "....Does anyone like to answer me please?"

And he'd go on and on like that all day. Nobody ever did answer the poor fellow except for David who got exasperated with the chap and told him in broken German to go and try somewhere else and who won the war anyway? Unfortunately Hans couldn't hear him since *Lakeland Rose* 's transmitter had difficulty reaching Boxingdale, never mind all the way across the North Sea to Hamburg.

One busy weekend we were all feeling a bit overworked and frantic and the CB was able to afford us some light relief. Captain Wright was away for the day so there was no-one to tell us to keep radio discipline. There was a party of army cadets exercising on Friars Fell - it's become a favourite haunt of the outdoor pursuit types - and by coincidence they were using our own operating channel. Nothing wrong with that, in those days we didn't have our own private channel. So every few minutes we'd overhear, loud and clear, calls like: "Hello green leader, hello green leader, this is red squad. Do you read me? Over."

David started getting cheesed off with all this nonsense so for a bit of amusement he decided to join in the conversation. After all, it's a bit boring driving *Lakeland Rose* past Friars Fell for most of the afternoon - there's nothing to see but trees. We all knew who it was because David's voice was familiar to us, but when those cadets heard it they hadn't a clue and assumed an officer had appeared on the scene since David had suddenly acquired a perfect Sandhurst accent.

"Hello red squadron, this is Blenheim. Over."
Blenheim? Who on earth was Blenheim?
"Hello Blenheim, this is red leader. Over."
"Red leader, this is Blenheim. What is your position, please?"

Sounding rather mystified, red leader gave his position.

"Thank you, red leader," came David's voice. "There's been a change of plan. Urgent you return to Sea Scout as soon as possible. Please acknowledge. Over."

We'd already worked out that Sea Scout was their observation post near the top of the fell. Red squadron had made a mock attack on the place and were now retreating through the woods."

"Say again, Blenheim." There was a tone of mild panic.

"Red leader, this is Blenheim. I repeat. Urgent you return to Sea Scout. Acknowledge. Over."

There was dead silence for a few moments; we all held our breath. Then Sea Scout came on the air. "Blenheim, Blenheim, this is Sea Scout. What's the problem? Over."

David remained equal to the situation. "Sea Scout, this is Blenheim. Information just received that you are to be attacked. I am calling Red Squadron to rendezvous with you urgently."

And then one of the brighter crewboys - young Martin Merryweather - cottoned on to what was happening. "Red leader, red leader, this is green squadron. Over."

"Go ahead, green. Over."

"Sir, the corporal's fallen and broken his leg.... over."

"What is your position, green? I say again, what is your position?"

A long pause. Then, "I'm not quite sure, sir."

David said: "Put a splint on it, then."

The crewboy continued: "Sir, he's screaming. The bone's sticking out."

General consternation. All kinds of voices started coming in over the CB - army men in a flat panic, drivers and crews all making their contribution. To lend a bit of realism to the situation, another crewboy (we all recognised his voice) started groaning very realistically into the microphone.

"Green squadron, I MUST have your position urgently. Is there anyone in your group who can read a map?"

Pause. Then, "No sir. Over."

There was a horrible silence, you could almost see the expression on the CO's face. And just at that point, someone quacked.

Yes, quacked. A genuine, beautiful, duck's quack. *Quack, quack, cwaaarrk!* Instant mystification. And then a voice - so well disguised we never *did* discover whose it was - asked in a perfect American accent: "Say, are there any ducks on this lake?"

Silence again. And then David's voice came over the air.

This time he was speaking normally, gone were those impeccable Sandhurst tones. "One or two, I think."

"Green squadron, green squadron, this is Red Leader. What is your position? Over."

"Would they be teal or goldeneye?"

"Shelducks, I think, actually," I butted in, thinking back to the little boat I once drove.

"Wow! Shelducks, eh? That's just great. You wait while I write the folks back home..."

"Look, whoever you are, will you go to another channel, we've got an emergency back here."

"No you haven't." David's voice.

"What do you mean, we haven't? There's a man with a broken leg. Please keep off the air while we call for assistance."

"Say, there's a duck over there, looks like it's got a broken wing. Can we not do something about it?"

"You could call the emergency services," said David. "Try the RSPB. Hang on a minute, I'll try and get their number."

"For God's sake will you get off the air? We're trying to call the emergency services ourselves!" said Sandhurst.

"Listen, you guys playing at soldiers.... a duck with a broken wing has as much right to first aid as a guy with a broken leg...."

A chorus of "Hear, hear!" followed by a prolonged "Quaarrk!"

When the cacophony had died down there was a pause and someone said: "This is green squadron. There's no-one here with a broken leg. Over."

A long pause during which teeth were audibly gnashed. Then: "Look, you jokers, I don't know what the hell you think you're playing at, but by the Lord Harry when I get down to you, you have my solemn promise that every single one of you will be personally sorted by me."

Silence. We boatmen knew when to keep quiet. The officer might have had a direction-finder in any case. Not that that would help him much, though - a boat is a moving target.

Ten seconds later David came on the air again in his normal voice, all professional, and the rest of us took our cue from him. "*Lakeland Rose* to *Pegasus*. Are you going astern of that cruiser, Geoff? I'll pass you port to port."

And *Pegasus* replied, "*Pegasus* to *Lakeland Rose*. A big Roger on that. Over and out."

We never heard anything more about the army manoeuvres

incident, but it certainly livened up an otherwise boring Saturday afternoon. Not that Saturday afternoons are boring in themselves, usually quite the opposite because there are plenty of weekend sailors about to keep us launch drivers on our toes, but on that particular Saturday there was a flat calm and not even the Birblemere Sailing Club were making much headway. We did, however, get some feedback about correct radio procedure.

Apparently it is the habit of the various inspectors, bureaucrats and other minor officials to listen in on other people's radio conversations. This is in order to pull people up for breaking the rules which the said officials are so fond of inventing - like not discussing religion or politics or not even using bad language.

Anyway, one of these inspectors had evidently overheard part (or perhaps all) of our dialogue with the army cadets that afternoon, and in due course an official-looking envelope appeared on Captain Wright's desk telling him to get his drivers sorted out. There was also a fancy brochure about a one-day course which you could take in correct operation and procedure in marine-band VHF. This would mean everyone taking a day off work to go down to Liverpool.

At first Captain Wright almost exploded, but then after thinking about it for a while he realised it wasn't such a bad idea after all since it meant that we could have our own private channel. No more interruptions from people in cars asking each other which direction to take, no more housewives asking their husbands when they'll be home for tea, and no more compulsive talkers from the CB clubs rabbitting away about smokeys, handles, twigs and all the rest of their ridiculous jargon. After all, we had our job to do, but they were only playing. And goodbye to Hans and his friends baying across the airwaves from Germany, goodbye to orienteering groups counting all their runners back, and goodbye to army cadets on exercise.

Because don't forget - as long as we could hear them, they could hear us, and if there was one thing Captain Wright hated above everything else, it was that outsiders might get an idea of how B.&L.L.S. operated.

Anyway, a few weeks later a salesman came round offering a load of marine-band radios on a special deal, and so inspired was Captain Wright by the fellow's oratory that he agreed to buy the lot. As a result of this we all had to go down to Liverpool on a one-day course to get our licences as fully qualified marine VHF radio operators. The firm hired a minibus and off we all went to Beatle-land. Well actually, we didn't see a great deal of Liverpool (which was perhaps a mercy, remarked David, who had a poor opinion of cities in any case) but we did learn a great deal about how to deal with emergencies at sea.

Indeed, that seemed to be what the course was all about: we spent an entire afternoon calling MAY-DAY to each other on practice radios but by the end of the day.... boy, could we handle an emergency! They didn't half din it into us: Switch to the emergency channel, give your Mayday call three times, the name of your boat three times, and then your position. After that, if there was still time before you sank, you could tell the world what was actually wrong.

I used to spend entire summer afternoons on Birblemere after that just worrying what I would actually do if there were a *real* emergency, and would I get it all right?

"MAYDAY! MAYDAY! MAYDAY! This is PEGASUS, PEGASUS, PEGASUS. Papa, Echo, Golf, Alpha, Sierra, Oscar, Sierra." (Yes, you had to spell it out that way, feeling more like a Panda patrol car than a ship in distress). "My position is Birblemere, two hundred yards south-west of Shuttleworth Point. Repeat, Birblemere, two hundred yards south-west of Shuttleworth Point. I am carrying sixty passengers. I have been in collision with a speedboat. I am holed amidships and am taking in water. I am also on fire. I have some casualties."

It just didn't bear thinking about.

You might now be forgiven for thinking that we were all properly organised with our marine band VHFs and there would be no more musical performances from Captain Wright at the end of the pier. Not a bit of it!

For one thing, Captain Wright, who had accompanied us all to Liverpool in the minibus, had disdained to take the radio operator's course in preference to taking Mrs Wright shopping. So that he still handled the radio like the old CB toy, while the rest of us chatted away in truly professional manner, which resulted in some occasional confusion. Radio procedure is not like talking on a telephone, for instance. You have to end each bit of conversation with the word "Over". This does not mean: "I've finished speaking." It means: "Over to you." And when the conversation is finished you have to say: "Out." You may NOT say "Over and out" because this is obviously meaningless. Even worse, you must NEVER say "Roger." This simply brands you as an amateur.

There is one peculiar thing about radio conversations - sorry, 'correspondence' as the professionals call it. The person speaking may say something which is perfectly intelligible in ordinary conversation; but the person receiving may hear something entirely different. Nobody knows why this is so, but it happens. For instance, there is not much difficulty in distinguishing 'port' and 'starboard', but 'north' and 'south' tend to come out much the same, which adds to the confusion in the bay. And as for *Pegasus* and *Crocus* - well just forget it. The confusion became so great we had to rechristen one boat *Peggy* and the other *Croak*. And they've remained that way ever since.

Another hazard to which we drivers are prone is picking up the wrong microphone. Don't forget we now had *two* mikes on the dashboard in front of us: one for giving commentaries into, the other for ship-to-ship communication. And it's very easy, in the heat of the moment, to pick up the wrong one. I suppose it's confusing enough for the passengers to be suddenly asked which pier they're supposed to be landing at; but that's nothing to giving a full commentary on the length and breadth of Birblemere to the Liverpool coastguard, which was what happened to me one afternoon. Not only was I using the wrong mike, I was even on the wrong channel! A very calm and unflustered voice thanked me politely for my information, and then suggested I try another channel. I was so embarrassed I went off the air for the rest of the afternoon.

CHAPTER 13. Across the Lake and Into the Trees

Summer doesn't last all year, and every season comes to an end - and a good thing too, some might say, David Duckworth in particular. You've already seen what happens to us in the winter, but my earliest years with Bulswick & Lake Launch Services were not all spent varnishing boats in a freezing boathouse. Most of us were simply given two weeks' wages and told to fend for ourselves. If any survived to the following Easter, we were taken on again.

Some of us chose exile in distant climes and travelled in foreign parts, to return six months later brown as berries and full of exotic tales of Mexico or the Philippines; some remained at home, starving in garrets, pale and unseen; while yet others were lucky enough to find employment - in which latter group I found myself.

My new employers were Fox and Fungus, and described themselves as forestry consultants. Messrs. Fox & Fungus had actually passed away many, many years ago, but the firm had carried on unchanged; unchanged in pay, in working conditions and in its general attitude to its employees, which made B.&L.L.S. seem in comparison like model employers of a new and permissive era.

My new bosses were 18th-century, antediluvian! You could even be sacked if you forgot to touch your cap to the foreman. However, they were the only alternative to the dole, so thither we had to go. Christmas was near, and orders for Christmas trees were beginning to pile up in the firm's in-tray.

Boating and forestry are actually not all that far removed from each other, for forestry is another 'labour of love' occupation, attracting those who want to be close to the land and get away from civilisation. You cannot get much farther from civilisation than digging up thousands of young (and prickly) Norway Spruce - Xmas trees to you - on a remote fellside, lashed by torrential rain or sleet in the semi-darkness of mid-December. Conditions there were so awful they can't have had it much worse in the trenches. In fact the only difference between us and the Western Front is we weren't being shot at. We used to say, when tea-break was over and it was back into the elements, "Right lads - over the top!"

So many of us had worked for Messrs. Fox & Fungus that it became something of a tradition amongst local boatmen. Even Captain Wright himself had laboured his statutory term over there; his father had probably been in bond to them. It was an apprenticeship to test endurance, develop leadership, build character.... you couldn't really call yourself a boatman unless you had spent at least one winter digging up Christmas trees - and planting fresh ones in the New Year.

To get there, to reach that remote plantation in the trackless wastes of Friars Fell, we had to catch the first ferry of the day, which left at some ungodly hour like six am, which of course in December was in the middle of the night. You would wake up with your alarm shrilling away, hear the endless drumming of rain in the street, grab a thermos of coffee, and stagger out into the wet, pitch darkness. Down at the lakeside, as we huddled in the tiny shelter waiting for the boat, the wind came whistling down the lake, the rain-squalls beat horizontally against the window, Birblemere looked at its most inhospitable. How remote seemed those dreamy days of summer - the calm, shimmering waters, the blue sky, the green and silent forest. Even driving a boat like *Wizard* seemed delightful in comparison!

Charlie Charcake used to cycle to work each day. One dark morning, obviously still drowsy from sleep, he arrived late at the ferry slipway and, noticing that the boat had already arrived and was waiting for him with ramp extended, continued pedalling and so cycled right down the slipway into the lake. For in fact the ferry had not only arrived, it had already set off again with the rest of us on board, all watching Charlie's predicament with increasing interest. When he was in the water and cycling up to his thighs, Charlie realised his faux pas, turned round and cycled all the way back home again before his trousers froze.

There were many comments regarding this affair. Had Charlie cycled after the ferry in the hope that he might catch it up? Had he intended cycling underwater right across the lake, emerging ahead of the boat at the other side? We shall never know because he decided to spend the rest of the day thawing out in the Black Cormorant, drank himself senseless and subsequently claimed to have no recollection of the incident.

Job number one on arriving at field HQ halfway up the blasted heath was to chop firewood and light an ancient stove. It would just be blazing nicely by the time daylight crept upon us, when we crawled out of the little shack which was our daytime accommodation and set off to work.

Job number two was to fill the kettle from a small beck and stand it on top of the stove. With luck it would be boiling by the time our first tea-break arrived. If inclement weather prevailed we would stop indoors all day and either read or play chess by candlelight, so it was not too bad after all. That was until the management had a brainwave and bought us all a set of waterproofs, after which there was no excuse for dodging work when it was pouring with rain.

Occasionally a deer would find its way into our little plantation of Norway spruce in spite of the high fence surrounding them. Swift action is then called for, otherwise the deer will eat all the tops off the young trees, and customers don't like a Christmas tree without a top to put the fairy on. So off we all went on a deer hunt, leaping and bounding through those rows of young trees in pursuit of a beautiful and graceful animal whose enormous, effortless leaps left us looking quite ridiculous. The sheer speed at which deer can travel through knee-high grass and densely packed trees has to be seen at close quarters to be appreciated.

We did, however, have a plan of campaign. The others all lined up at one end of the nursery, and slowly and noisily advanced through the rows of Christmas trees whilst I crept round the perimeter to the other end and advanced towards them. The idea was for them to drive the deer towards me, and I was supposed to ambush it. Have you ever tried to rugger-tackle a deer bounding through the undergrowth at 30 mph? Well, it wasn't easy, but I tackled him all the same, and he kicked me so hard that I had to let him go. I had hoof-marks on my ribs for a week afterwards, and it transpired that the regular forestry workers always test the nerve and gullibility of newcomers in this fashion whenever a deer gets into the plantation.

Next time, I decided on a better plan: I would drive the deer while everybody else could bushwhack it, but the others demurred. There was, it was explained to me, a much easier method. We open the gate wide, make a lot of noise to frighten it and then retire into the hut for twenty minutes. When we come out the deer will have stopped panicking, thought it all out and left, although without closing the gate behind it.

I learned quite a lot about trees before returning to boating, with a sigh of relief, the following spring. I also learned the difference between Norway and Sitka spruce. If you think Christmas trees are spiky, try handling the latter without gloves - it doesn't have needles but steel spikes, and the following Christmas I laughed myself silly at a big party where the host had unwittingly obtained a Sitka spruce instead of Norway, and had severely lacerated himself trying to decorate it.

In addition I now knew what it was to have an hour's hard, uphill walk over rough ground, carrying tools and equipment, in all weathers, before the day's work had even started.

And so back to the boats. One summer, amongst the annual gang of young cabin-boys who come to spend a season or two working on the launches, we had some fully paid-up, 24-carat wim-wams, whose gullibility we tested as far as it would go. One of them was fishing about over the side of the pier with a net that we keep for retrieving objects dropped in the lake, such as ladies' shoes. (It's amazing, by the way, how many ladies actually drop a shoe in the water when boarding or leaving a boat). He eventually came up with an old beer can, and we told the unimaginative youth that if he conveyed this relic to the bar of the Cormorant, he would be given a small sum of money for it.

Off he went clutching his mud-encrusted relic and duly presented it to the barman, saying whence he came and why. The barman, being an old acquaintance of the boatmen, immediately saw through this little story, and told the boy that unfortunately they didn't stock this particular brand of beer, but that if he went to the cocktail bar in the exclusive Devonshire Hotel, the staff there would be only too happy to pay him. The head barman of the Devonshire Hotel, on being confronted with a scruffy little boy demanding money for a mouldy old beer can, cuffed the lad soundly and sent him packing with a warning never to darken the doors of that illustrious establishment again.

Another youth was sent off to the firm's winter workshop and boatstore to find a gentleman by the name of Old Scrotham to ask him for some green oil to put in the starboard navigation light and red oil for the port lamp. He also had to fetch two cans of elbow grease. Old Scrotham was the firm's wrinkled retainer. He was a friendly little man who looked after all the store-keeping and did all the odd jobs which always need doing. He had worked there since time immemorial, pottering around the place for a long as anyone could remember - he was old when Bill Birblethwaite was a lad, and that's going back a few years.

He was also the only person in the firm who has never been out on the lake. He disliked water intensely but loved all the appurtenances of boating, and he'll probably still be looking after the place when we've all retired and the next generation of boatmen are coming on. Paint, varnish, oars, shackles - Old Scrotham guards and hoards and supplies everything we need, including a lot of things we don't.

Our old retainer recognised the request for coloured oils for coloured lamps as being a typical boatman's joke, but being a kindly soul he took pity on the youth, and led him on a tour of the shed, explaining what everything was for and how all the machines worked. Our shed is something of a museum as well as a boat store; we have ancient tools, primitive machinery installed at about the same time as Old Scrotham arrived on the scene, relics of boats long disappeared, and each with a story attached to it. No-one ever throws these things out, however desperate we are for space: such is the boatman's sentimental attachment to the past.

The boy returned from his conducted tour of this Aladdin's cave seeing the world of boats in a different light and with a greater appreciation and understanding. He had, however, brought neither coloured oil nor elbow grease back with him, and was therefore sent off to the nearby café for half a dozen mugs of P-Squared's tea.

The old café on the waterfront had changed hands. Dora had retired and we boatmen missed her a great deal. But you don't get rich out of providing soup and tea and coffee virtually free to your main customers, and anyway the greedy landlord had put up the rent by several hundred percent, so Dora had decided to call it a day. The business was now run by a small firm of caterers who - unforgivably - came from outside Bulswick. Admittedly only from a few miles away, but that was quite enough to get them classified as "off-comers". The personal touch had vanished, and so had cheap prices and specially prepared boatmen's soup.

All was not lost, however, because at the other end of the beach, and across the road, was another café owned and run by a gentleman named Philip Poole, hence his nickname, "P-Squared". We all called him that, even the various locally-recruited girls whom he employed for the boatmen to flirt with - most considerate! If you took your mug to the kitchen door and crossed his palm with silver, P-Squared would fill it up with tea; and such tea! P-Squared's tea killed all known germs; it was often used to clean brasses, and was reputed to cure rheumatism if rubbed vigorously on the affected part. You could even drink it.

It was whilst we were waiting for tea to arrive, and cursing the boy for being slow, that we heard a roar from the main pier like that of a maddened bull. We all turned to see the cause of this disturbance, and it turned out to be Doug MacBride enraging Captain Wright. He often did this when he was in a mood, and his offence on this occasion was to try and repeat his famous flying leap onto a departing launch. The launch was *Pandora*, and Doug had just set it astern at the start of a cruise, then climbed out again, to follow the launch down the pier. The idea was to jump back on board at the very last minute before he ran out of pier, but the prospect of a launch under way and filled with fifty passengers and no driver so incensed Captain Wright that he would execute a war dance there and then.

Captain Wright had no room to talk, however, for if we were to believe everything we were told, in his younger days he had been a bit of a tearaway. A former skipper of *Mallard* (he had driven her on her maiden voyage) he had been the terror of all the sailing boats on Birblemere - even worse than Boxer Bill, if the truth were known. He used to attack a flock of dinghies like a rabid sheepdog, harrying them, turning them this way and that, then separating a couple from the rest and worrying them for a while before letting them return to their fellows.

Let's not forget the time, either, when he smashed all the crockery in a cabin cruiser, driving so close and so fast that his wash caused the vessel to rock with such violence as to spill every moveable object onto the deck. Well, it was their own fault for not putting all the cups away in cupboards. And there was the occasion when he drove flat out past one of the boatyards and his wash caused one of the cruisers berthed there to rise up and settle down fair and square on one of the low piers. It was Captain Wright himself who answered the phone when they rang up to complain ten minutes later. "Good!" he told them. "I'll see if I can wash it off again next time round!"

He used to enjoy telling us these witty little stories, but he didn't tell us the one when he was heaving lustily on a rope to pull a couple of launches towards the pier, the innermost one having departed on a cruise. They were heavy boats, and he was really putting his back into it - when the rope broke. It was old and frayed, but he didn't see that, took two steps backwards off balance, let out a terrific roar, and disappeared from view off the other side of the pier into *Skua*, which was just at that moment coming alongside.

He landed amongst *Skua's* astonished passengers who cushioned his fall, and showered them with bank notes and loose change from the money bag. His deputy was on the scene in seconds to start retrieving the money, scrabbling around on the deck on his hands and knees, groping under seats, round passengers' ankles, completely oblivious to the loud groans from Captain Wright, who was lying spread over three seats with a broken back. Actually he was only bruised, and it turned out the moans were caused more from thinking about all the loose change now rolling about in the oily bilges, than from mere physical distress.

There was an occasion one season when we had policemen driving boats. Three young officers in particular had started coming down in their spare time to help out, and it soon reached the point where half the local constabulary were messing about on the lake when out of uniform. Eventually the inspector had to put a stop to this particular pastime, on the grounds that the police station would only open on weekdays if this were to be the pattern of future duties. Perhaps it was just as well they were stopped, because as any small-boat sailor will tell you, there are two things you must NEVER take on a boat. One is an umbrella, the other is a policeman, for both will become tangled up in everything in a very short time.

A young constable called Alastair did everything he could to live up to this saying. They put him on *Wizard*, which was rather unkind - perhaps he had once given a shareholder's wife a parking ticket - but then *somebody* had to drive it. As he was crossing the lake a passenger sitting in front asked P.C. Alastair a question, and on leaning forward to answer he pulled on the wheel, which promptly came off its mountings and crashed to the deck. He fumbled frantically with chains and cables, but couldn't put it all together again, and there was the shore looming nearer and nearer. In the end all his police training and initiative came to the rescue, and he calmed down sufficiently to realise that if he put the engine out of gear and stopped it, he would drift about instead of heading out of control to certain destruction. This he did, and *Wizard* wallowed helplessly for half an hour until picked up by another launch and towed back to port.

Sooner or later we all have a breakdown. My own occurred when I was driving *Mallard* - once the fleet flagship. I had a Jolliways coach party on board, en route from Bulswick to Boxingdale, where their coach was due to collect them in a couple of hours' time, always providing that the coach driver went to the right end of the lake. It has happened, you will not be surprised to learn, that a launch full of passengers has arrived at one end of the lake, dropped them off and set off back for Bulswick, only to find that the coach driver had gone to the opposite end of the lake. The coach passengers are well and truly stranded, not knowing where their coach is, not even knowing where they are, and without a clue as to what they should do. It takes a good while before everything is sorted out.

Anyway, there we were, cruising sedately along in a fairly deserted part of Birblemere with a typical party of Americans doing Britain in a day and asking every conceivable sort of question, when the engine stopped. No warning - it just died away - fuel blockage, probably. At the time, I was dealing with the inevitable querist. "What sort of engine has she got, driver?" You have to be careful when answering this one, or you'll end up talking about engines for the rest of the cruise, so I parried the thrust with: "A blue one, sir." This stops them dead in their tracks.

I could have added at that point, "Not a very reliable one." However, since the wind was gusting a bit, I thought it prudent to drop anchor. The passengers looked a little alarmed, so I assured them I wasn't abandoning ship and leaving them to their fate, just climbing onto the bow in order to lower the anchor.

It's a funny thing about anchors: regardless of the size of boat, they all seem to be the same shape and size, except that the cables are thicker on the larger vessels. So I heaved it over the side, watching the cable rattle out as it followed the shank over the gunwhale and down, down into the murky depths. You are probably chuckling to yourselves thinking the silly fool's forgotten to tie the end on, but you're wrong, that's the very first thing you do before you let go, secure the end of the cable to a cleat. We all remember what happened to Duncan Preedie when he broke down once in *Suzanne:* an expensive anchor disappeared overboard, followed very promptly by a hundred feet of chain, which left him looking very foolish indeed, and drifting into the shore. *Suzanne's* anchor and cable are still out there in the depths of Birblemere if anyone wants to fish them out.

I think if that ever happened to me I would quietly follow the cable over the side. How do you face your passengers after losing the anchor? For don't forget they will all be sitting there in the cabin, watching your every move. Twenty minutes later help arrived in the shape of *Pandora*, whose grinning skipper hove to alongside and jovially asked if we had stopped to do a spot of fishing. So we secured side by side, I hauled up the anchor cable which was covered in green weed, while the anchor had obviously buried itself fifty feet below us in something very nasty indeed judging from the stuff oozing and dripping off its flukes. Coleridge got it about right when he said:

"*Yea, slimy things did crawl with legs*
Upon the slimy sea."

So there you are, that's it - that's what life was like for a Lake District launch driver many years ago - or perhaps not all that many after all. Those are just a few of the countless incidents which go to make up everyday life in the Lakes; just the tip of the iceberg, as it were. But don't think that's the end of the story. Far from it - this is only the beginning. Funny incidents happen all the time, in every walk of life, and we hope they always will. After all, what would life be without a little comedy?

The following title is also published by the Orinoco Press:-

TALES AND LEGENDS OF WINDERMERE

by Peter Nock

£2.40   40 pp., illus.

This little volume deals with authentic ghost stories, legends, folklore, local history, etc. connected with Lake Windermere in the past. These include:

The Crier of Claife

A horrific ghost haunted the Windermere ferryman to his death, and was subsequently banished by a priest to the wooded slopes of Claife Heights.

The Calgarth Skulls

Myles Philipson coveted a plot of land belonging to an elderly couple and contrived to have them executed. Their skulls returned to haunt him and his descendants - right through to the present day.

Robin the Devil

How Robert Philipson of Long Holme rode on horseback into Kendal Parish Church in pursuit of his Roundhead enemy - a true story from the time of the Civil War.

Drenched Souls

In 1635 the Windermere ferry sank during a gale with the loss of 48 lives, including guests returning from a wedding at Hawkshead.

Two Black Hands

'Colonel' John Bolton of Storrs Hall, a ruthless businessman and slave trader, had a bloodthirsty past which eventually caught up with him.

Belle Isle

The story of the island's famous round house which became the holiday home of Isabella Curwen, the orphaned heiress of Workington Hall, who ran away to marry her childhood playmate.

ISBN 0 9514778 1 1